THE AMISH COWBOY'S HOME

AMISH COWBOYS OF MONTANA
BOOK VI

ADINA SENFT

Cover design by Carpe Librum Book Design. Images used under license. "O Blessed Hope," words by Eliza E. Hewitt, music by William J. Kirkpatrick, now in the public domain. *"Er hat ein Weib genommen,"* translated by Shelley Adina Senft Bates.

The Amish Cowboy's Home / Adina Senft—1st ed.

ISBN 978-1-950854-86-8 R111223

❀ Created with Vellum

CAST OF CHARACTERS
THE AMISH COWBOY'S HOME

The Montana Millers. They believe in faith, family, and the land. They'll need all three when love comes to the Circle M!

The Amish Cowboy's Home combines a family wedding with Christmas—two events guaranteed to bring lots of people into the house. I'm including here a list of the three families staying on the Circle M this Christmas. Only Naomi Miller can keep track of them all!

The Montana Millers on the Circle M Ranch

- Reuben and Naomi Glick Miller
- Daniel and Lovina Wengerd Lapp Miller, Joel
- Adam Miller and Kate Weaver (engaged)
- Zach Miller
- Malena Miller and Alden Stolzfus (courting)
- Noah and Rebecca Miller King
- Joshua and Sara Fischer Miller, Nathan

The New Mexico Millers

- Rachel Zook Miller (widow of Marlon Miller, brother of Reuben)
- Tobias Miller, Gracie and Benny
- Susanna Miller
- Gideon Miller
- Seth Miller

The Prince Edward Island Kuepfers

- Lorne and Salome Glick Kuepfer
- Caleb Kuepfer
- Emily Kuepfer
- Jacob Kuepfer
- Aaron Kuepfer
- Jenny Kuepfer

IN THIS SERIES
AMISH COWBOYS OF MONTANA

THE AMISH COWBOY'S HOME

MOUNTAIN HOME, MONTANA

Two weeks before Christmas

"Do you think Ruby Wengerd will let me give her a ride home from singing?"

It was church Sunday, hosted today at the Circle M Ranch, and David Yoder had come down to the basement with Zachariah Miller to stoke the woodstove. It was twenty below outside, with a warmup predicted later in the week that would probably mean snow. But the heat from the stove was conducted upstairs by two battery-powered fans, keeping the house comfortable. And the crowd of *Youngie* who had stayed after church for visiting and the singing were doing plenty to keep the house warm, with all the talking and laughing.

To cover his surprise at his friend's question, Zach opened the flue, then the stove door, and tossed in a couple more quarter cuts of fir. "I didn't know you were interested in her. When did that happen?"

David hesitated, which wasn't normal for him. He thought about things in advance, so usually had an answer ready. His brother Calvin was the opposite—he hardly ever thought about things before he did or said them, just let them fly. "During this morning's preaching."

Which had been the last text of the year—Matthew 24 and 25. Two weeks from now they'd begin the new worship year with Christmas, and the birth of Christ, one of Zach's favorite texts. But that was in the future. Here in the present, he had questions.

"So the preaching on the end of the world made you think of Ruby?" he asked dryly. "I wouldn't mention that to her. She might get the wrong idea." He closed the door, but kept the flue open until the current of air caused the wood to catch.

"*Neh*, I won't, but I have to admit it got me thinking. I'm twenty-four and the only girl I've courted lately was Kate Weaver. Then Adam scooped her out from under my nose. I thought about Rebecca before that, but there was the whole thing with her being courted by two men last spring, and anyhow, next week she and Noah are getting married. It feels like if I don't get serious, I'm going to miss out and all the good ones will be spoken for."

What did Dave consider a "good one"? Kate and Rebecca couldn't be more different, from skills in the home to personality. But every sensible Amish person considered a potential spouse's spiritual service to *der Herr* as one of the most important things about them.

He hoped Dave meant it that way, too. He also wasn't about to ask.

"And so you thought of Ruby." Zach closed the flue and throttled down the air intake, then turned his attention to David. The man tended to confide in him about girls and romance, maybe because Zach had a reputation for being "the quiet one" in the Miller family. But probably it was because no one in his right mind would confide in Calvin, who reminded Zach of a funnel. Pour something in his ear and it came straight out his mouth, usually at the most embarrassing moment possible.

"Well, why not? She's the bishop's daughter. A man can't do better than that."

Zach's face scrunched a little, but it could be blamed on the heat of the stove. He stepped back, out of the orange glow, so that his face was in shadow. "But do you like her? Think the same way about things? Enjoy the same kind of stuff?"

"I don't know any of that, do I? Not until I court her. I figure I have to do better than Calvin, at least. She turned him down flat."

"*Calvin* asked Ruby out? Your brother?"

"Don't sound so amazed. He wants to get married. She isn't seeing anyone. So he gave it a try. The big ox—they have nothing in common. But I don't know if I do, either."

"Dave, you've known her all your life." So had he.

But Calvin Yoder? It was all he could do not to shake his head. The truth was, he felt a little bit protective of Ruby—who was painfully shy, and quiet as a result. But she was a hard worker, and the first person to come and help when you needed it. Just yesterday, she'd come over to help with the food for Rebecca and Noah's wedding, which was just nine days away. Mamm was getting pretty stressed about everything being ready on time, so more helping hands for the baking and preparations had been a gift.

Ruby was like that. A gift that hardly anyone seemed to notice—until she wasn't there.

Had it really taken preaching about the end of the world to remind Dave Yoder that she, of all other young women, was missing from his life?

Zach realized that Dave wasn't going back upstairs, even though they heard the chairs scraping on the wood floors, a sure sign that everyone was sitting down for the second round of singing after the snack. He had to give him the reply he'd asked for a minute ago.

"All you can do is ask her if she'd like a ride." He kept his voice even. Easy. The voice of a friend. "Though you kind of missed your moment to work up to it, coming down here instead of offering to get her a drink."

Dave clapped a hand to his forehead. "I should have done that! Now someone else probably has. I'm going to try anyway." Without another word, he galloped up the stairs to the kitchen.

Zach let out a long breath. His mind shouted that he should have stopped him, that he should have galloped up there himself and warned Ruby that the other Yoder brother had set his sights on her. But it was none of his business. Besides, if she'd turned Calvin down, then surely she'd be able to do the same for Dave. The younger of the two was a nice guy, but a little too strict and focused on appearances for Zach's taste. He hadn't forgotten what Adam had confided to him when Dave had made a play for Kate Weaver.

"He implied that there was something underhanded about her traveling as far as Colorado with the King brothers when she was planning to go back to Whinburg Township," Adam had said, frowning. "Like she was going to get up to something with Andrew the minute she was alone with him. Kate didn't care much for that."

As it turned out, Andrew had wanted to get up to something with *her*, and she'd sent him backward off a log for his pains. And now Andrew, the middle King brother, too handsome for his own good, was out east, courting Kate's sister Elizabeth. A match made in heaven, if ever there was one.

Zach stood in front of the stove, letting the heat toast him gently. The *gut Gott* had certainly been busy making matches in the valley over the last year or so. All his siblings had found love, one or two in ways that were miraculous, for sure and certain. Like Joshua and Sara, now happily living at the hay farm with their baby Nathan, full of plans for what they would do with their crop in the spring. Or even Rebecca, next week's bride, who had received a push from the mighty hand of *der Herr* and saved the life of Andrew, her future brother-in-law. What about his eldest brother Daniel, who still thanked *Gott* in his prayers every night that Lovina had been brought practically to his doorstep by that same mighty hand. None of the Millers believed it was by chance. To a person of faith, *Gott* was the author of everything that happened in the lives of His children. The Creator of beauty. The grand design of life was His alone.

It was breathtaking when you thought about it. That He would even consider a life as small as Zach's, for instance, a cowboy pretty much restricted to these spreading acres, as significant enough for His direction and care.

How long, O Lord? Zach hardly dared to think it, but the Psalmist's words had already formed in his mind. *How long until it's my turn and You show me the one You mean for me? I'm the last one in my family to find love, and it's a mighty lonely place to be. I'm ready and willing, Lord, when in Your infinite wisdom and love You turn Your attention to me.*

He bowed his head in humility.

And when the heat from the stove made it too hot to put off going upstairs any longer, he loped up the stairs and emerged into the kitchen.

"You must have put a lot of wood on that fire." Ruby Wengerd turned from the dishes to give him a smile.

But all Zach could see was Dave Yoder standing there with a dish towel in his hands, drying plates and handing them to Zach's sister Malena to put away. Just the way a member of the family would.

The sight of them at the sink irritated him so much that it was all he could do to produce an answering smile. He joined the *Youngie* in the other room as fast as he could, just in time for the second verse of "I Shall Know Him."

RUBY WENGERD WRESTLED DOWN HER DISAPPOINTMENT and turned back to the dishes. Zach Miller had something on his mind, and she shouldn't take it personally. But she'd give a lot to know what he and Dave Yoder had been talking about down there in the basement that would have resulted in the astonishing sight of Dave picking up a dish towel and offering to help her and Malena.

Malena was no slouch. From the expression in her eyes, she'd just got a little idea—one that was completely wrong.

Never had dishes been done so quickly and with so little conversation. But then, people didn't seem to expect her to talk very much. Which was a relief, because they sure expected a lot from every other aspect of her life.

The *Gmee* had gathered to choose a new bishop when she was ten. And *der Herr* had seen to it that Dat had found the short piece of hay in the hymnbook. Then, Mamm and Dat had explained to her what that meant. *Der Herr* had chosen Dat to lead the two churches that formed the Siksika Valley district, and he would be gone to the other church on the eastern side of Mountain Home every other Sunday.

It had taken quite a while to realize there was a lot more to the task *Gott* had set him for the rest of his life than she had ever been aware of before. A task that sometimes required prayer and tears. A task that might take him away from them for more than just alternate Sundays—especially if there was snow and he couldn't get home.

But what she really hadn't known then was what it would mean to her and her siblings. Her eldest brother, Peter, was married by then, and Victor hadn't been far behind. So they saw Dat more as an example of what could be their portion some-day, as married men. Her two sisters, Lilian and Anna Rose, had been in their teens. Knowing what she knew now, Ruby could only imagine the changes that being the new bishop's daughters would have made in their lives. Mind you, she loved her broth-ers-in-law and believed her sisters had made *gut* choices.

But though she had grown into her new place, in a way, Ruby never found it easier. Because while everyone was equal in the eyes of *Gott*, humans were fallible and inclined to put people in order. Bishop, bishop's wife, bishop's daughter.

She and Mamm had to be the most unfit for such a place of anyone in the whole valley. Ellie and Susan Bontrager, on the other hand, would have been perfect ... but, well, *Gott* never made mistakes. She had to admit that Mamm—so painfully shy, so self-effacing—was such a force for good when she got down on her knees that Ruby had the uncomfortable feeling that maybe it was only she, Ruby, having so much trouble filling her place.

Even after all this time.

When the dishes were done, she and Malena and Dave

went out to the living room. Ruby found a place on the end of one bench, and for the next hour, kept her eyes on her songbook, even for the ones like "Country Roads" that everyone knew by heart. Dave Yoder was up to something, she just knew it, and was trying to communicate it by catching her eye.

There weren't all that many *Youngie* in the valley—it only took four tables to seat them. Dat did not hold to the *Ordnung* of some districts, where girls sat at one table, boys at another —no, they were allowed to share tables, boys on one side, girls on the other. She'd sat as far from Dave as she could, but still, every time she glanced up, he was giving her puppy-dog eyes.

She had a feeling he wanted to give her a ride home, too.

Well, what's wrong with that? He's nice, and is part owner of Yoder's Variety Store with his father and Calvin. You could do worse.

Worse than being Calvin's sister-in-law?

Dave is nothing like Calvin.

Or—

As though her eyes and her thoughts had a will of their own, they found Zach Miller at the other table with the accuracy of a homing pigeon. No one was like him. People said he was quiet, but really it was because he was a thinker. He saw the world as a place of beauty, if his drawings were anything to go by. He'd shown them to her once, and they'd taken her breath away.

"Aw, it's just a bunch of doodles," he said, and closed the notebook. "Anybody can do this."

Anybody named Zach Miller, that is. She couldn't draw a straight line with a ruler.

An hour later, the singing came to an end, and there was a buzz of good-byes and a scramble for boots and scarves and coats. Ruby did her best to vanish in plain sight, but she wasn't nearly as good at it as Rebecca Miller used to be.

Because she was the bishop's daughter, and people's eyes were on her. All the time.

However, she did manage to get her coat and everything else on while evading Dave at the same time—quite a feat. She even made it out the door and halfway down the front stairs before she heard him call her name.

"Ruby, wait up."

Before the fog of her breath had cleared in the cold air, he had joined her. "Can I give you a ride home? It's awful cold— no night for walking."

"It's all right," she said. "Once I get on the highway, it's only a quarter mile to our lane."

"A quarter mile at twenty below won't give you frostbite, but I'd still feel better if you came with me in the buggy."

Oh, so it was a health matter and nothing else? Hmph. Then again, he was being kind, and Zach was nowhere to be seen, and what did it matter anyway?

"All right," she said. *"Denki."*

"It won't take a minute to hitch up. I'll see you in the lane."

No one would be so foolish as to climb into a boy's buggy right here by the steps, in full view of practically every single person in the valley. So like one or two other girls, she strolled down the lane into the shadows of the trees, berating herself for not simply saying no.

It was all Zach's fault. If he'd only notice her—think of her as more than a friend—then none of this would be happening.

In a few minutes, Dave's buggy rolled up beside her and he slid the passenger door open. "I have a blanket," he said.

Ruby didn't care for the notion of their legs side by side under the same blanket, sharing body heat. *"Denki,"* but I'm warm, and my coat is heavy."

To her relief, he didn't argue as he turned on to the highway. She barely had time to let her breath out, though, before he said, "I was thinking. Maybe we might sit together. You know, at the wedding."

Well if that wasn't as forward as a man could get! "Dave, you know as well as I do that it's the bride's prerogative to choose who sits together at supper."

He grinned. "And you know as well as I that a little bird can sing in the bride's ear beforehand. What do you say?"

She gathered her courage. "I don't think I'm ready to make such a statement in front of everyone. Especially my parents."

"A statement? Is that what it is? Not an opportunity to get to know one another?"

Was she really reduced to pointing out the obvious? "We've known each other all our lives."

Dave's horse picked up its pace, as if it, too, wanted to take her home quickly, the sooner to get to its warm barn. Dave pulled a little on the reins to slow it down. To draw out this quarter mile as long as he could.

Wunderbaar.

"There's a difference between knowing someone in church and at doings, and knowing them personally," he said. "For instance, what do you know about me?"

She resigned herself to the next few minutes. "I know that you're a *gut Bruder* to Sallie, Maryanne, and Lydia, and that your *mamm* is first cousin to Rose Stolzfus."

"That's my family. What about me?"

They were almost to the lane that led home. "I know that when you were little, you followed Calvin into every bit of mischief he got up to. And that sometimes you still do."

"I wouldn't call it mischief."

"What do you call the washing machine incident at Victor's wedding?"

"That wasn't us—it was the Zook brothers. And that was years ago. Do you think a bunch of kids could get a washing machine out on to a frozen lake all by ourselves?"

"You helped."

Dave grinned. "*Ja*, we sure did. Your brother thought he was so smart, getting that machine for his wife. He should have known better than to show it."

Maybe that was so, but Ruby still felt the criticism as though it had been directed at her. "He worked hard to be able to give her that. Converted it himself so it would run on the generator." And in doing so, he had discovered a skill he hadn't known he possessed. Now Victor and Janie lived on the east side of the valley and he did mechanical conversions full time, out of his shop in the barn.

Maybe it was time to turn the tables. "What do you know about me?" She kept her voice pleasant, all the while calculating how long it would take the horse to get to the house, now that they'd finally turned into the lane.

"I know that you're a faithful, quiet, obedient woman, like the one in Proverbs 31."

Had he ever actually read that chapter? "She might have been faithful, but she wasn't quiet and obedient. She was out there buying vineyards and selling linen, and sewing garments and planting crops."

"You sew and plant. And what does it say? *In her tongue is the law of kindness.* That fits you well."

All right, so maybe he had read it. "When I get a chance to speak," she said without thinking.

He drew up in front of the house. "What does that mean?"

"It means that ... I'm a quiet person. Sometimes it's because I'd rather keep my thoughts to myself. And sometimes it's because I can't get a word in edgewise."

He darted a look at her as if checking to see whether he ought to laugh or not. She couldn't help comparing him to Zach, who smiled often but didn't laugh much. When he did—when something struck him as funny—the whole room knew about it.

She treasured the times she'd managed to make him laugh.

"I like a quiet person," he said. "I'd like to think that maybe *I* could get a word in edgewise."

"But conversation is supposed to go two ways, be spontaneous, because you like the things the other person likes," she said. "And if you don't, you can say why without being laughed at or argued with."

"I hate when someone argues with me. When people argue at all," he admitted bluntly. The reins lay loose in his hands. Was that a sign that he didn't intend to try to kiss her good night? How soon could she get down?

"There," she said, doing her best to sound like a sister. "Something I didn't know about you. Because of Calvin?"

"*Neh*, because of the Bible. Paul says women should keep silence."

"In the churches," she pointed out. It was why Amish women were not called to the position of preacher, deacon, or bishop. "Not all the time."

"Quietness is an important quality in a woman, in church or out," he said. "My mother has many *gut* qualities, but that isn't one of them."

This was getting out of hand. Now his own mother didn't measure up to his high standards?

"But as the bishop's *Docher*, you would know—"

Ruby slid open the door with a scrape and got out. "*Denki* for the ride, Dave," she said. "But I don't think you should ask me a second time. We'll just remain friends, *nix*?"

"Wait—we've hardly said anything to each other. Aren't you going to invite me in?"

"It's twenty below. What about your horse?"

"I'll put her in the barn."

The weight of his expectations settled on her like a fog, making it almost impossible to move forward. But in her memory, she heard the sound of Andrew King going over backward off that log and landing with a *whoof* in the gravel.

"I don't think so," she said. "I'm going in now."

"But Ruby, I—"

"Now who's arguing?" she said sweetly, and ran up the steps into the warm welcome of the house.

VENTANA VALLEY, NM

❧ 2 ❧

FOUR WINDS RANCH
Friday, December 10

DEAR NAOMI AND REUBEN,

Thanks for your letter—and for the elk jerky. The boys like to carry it in their pockets when they're riding fence, to tide them over until mealtime. I suppose yours do, too. Never give a gift you can't use, as Marlon used to say.

While I know he's safe with God now, I sure do miss him. At times like this, when I want to talk over a decision, I picture him sitting across from me, nodding and listening hard in that way he had, head cocked like a robin. So maybe I'll talk it over with you two, since you're most concerned in it. I don't want to phone long distance. Sometimes writing it out helps the thinking process.

I'll just say it flat out—I want to sell the ranch and move back to the Siskita Valley.

There. I can see the two of you now, your eyes wide as you look at each other. It was just as much a surprise to me, too, when I woke up one summer morning with the certain knowledge that it was time to come home. Time to give up ranching and be closer to the family. We're nearly the last Amish in the Ventana Valley now, did you know? There were three families left in church, and one of them has gone back to Kentucky now. Our bishop is such a good friend that he and his family will stay as long as we do. But I know Betty wants to leave the high country and go back to Pennsylvania. It's just as cold there, but at least the soil will yield crops, and their eldest has a nice place with a Daadi Haus standing empty.

So, all that said, my question is, what can the New Mexico Millers do to keep food on the table when they become the Montana Millers?

As Tobias has pointed out more than once, I'm handy at managing a ranch, and a home, and cooking, but unless there's a market for chile sauce out there, that's pretty much the extent of my skills. I don't expect you need more than yourself, Reuben, to manage the books and stock on the Circle M. Especially not a woman staring down fifty like it was an ornery coyote.

When we're out there for Rebecca's wedding, maybe I can look around a bit. Tobias, Gideon, and Seth are experienced hands, so they'll find work easily, especially if I can get the stock and property sold by early spring. Susanna doesn't want to leave the ranch she's grown up on, but as I tell her, even a rock on a hill changes its position from year to year. Doesn't change the rock, just the way the sun falls on it. The sun will fall differently on us in Montana—if only because of the altitude. And the twins? Well, every day is an adventure for them. Between high spirits and the Holy Spirit, they're beginning to find their way after the loss of their mother. I'm not so certain about Tobias. His faithful heart will take longer to recover, I suspect. For his sake, new scenes and hard work will be the best medicine.

I'm looking forward to being with family again. Our kids would *probably laugh at my notions, but I want them to grow older together, have families close by, be in church together. I want Susanna especially to grow closer to your girls. Our district is so small she hasn't had much chance to form long-term female friendships—the kind we've had in our buddy bunches, Naomi, and still have. Her friendships have mostly been by letter.*

Speaking of, this is a long one, and my yellow pad is running out of sheets. I'll let this do for now.

With much love in Him,
Rachel

Monday, December 13

EVEN IN THE DEEPS OF WINTER, ZACH HAD WORK TO DO ON the ranch. With the wedding next week, and Christmas right after, the house was a whirlwind inside. Best to steer clear of it. Luckily, since church had been here this past Sunday, the house and outbuildings had been cleaned to within an inch of their lives. Now, Mamm was marshaling the twins for the cooking and baking, while Sara had brought Nathan over to play with little Deborah while she and Ruby loaded up Daniel's spring wagon with bedding and linens. It would all go down to Daniel and Lovina's house. While Aendi Rachel and Susanna would stay at the big house, her sons would fill the bedrooms at the newly completed house overlooking the river.

Zach wasn't certain who else among their extended family were coming for the wedding. Melvin and Carrie Miller in Whinburg Township had been invited, of course, but with Carrie so close to having her second baby, Melvin didn't want to take chances with a long trip. Zach had heard a rumor that some of Mamm's cousins were coming from the East Coast. He'd met that family when he was little at one of the relatives' weddings, but didn't remember them very well. Mamm had been delighted when the letter had come in response to the invitation, though. They, too, would stay at Daniel's, with the overflow going into the bunkhouse if needed.

Zach would never dream of saying out loud that the prospect of the ranch full to bursting with so many people made him want to run away. Daniel had his lookout up on the grazing allotment—Adam had his meadow over where his house would be—Joshua had the hay farm and his home with Sara. Maybe he should borrow one or more of those places to run to when things were crazy like this.

But today, no one was scheduled to arrive, and he was content to work on fixing the calving pen and getting it ready for February and March. You could pretty much guarantee that the mother cows would drop their calves on the wildest, stormiest night of the year. Sometimes they had a difficult birth, or the calf needed help with standing or nursing, and they would bring them in here where it was safe and warm, and no coyotes prowled in the howling dark looking for the weak and vulnerable.

The human door next to the big slider where the buggies came and went opened, admitting a slice of winter afternoon sunlight and the ropy form of his father.

"In the pen, Dat," he called.

"Adam with you?"

"No, he's out back, splitting wood. Hear him?" In the distance, the wood splitter growled and snarled as Adam reduced seasoned rounds of a fallen oak to useful lengths for the stove.

His father joined him, a hammer and a tin of nails in his

gloved hands. "Nice and quiet in here."

"This time next week, it won't be. Enjoy it now."

"Aw, it's not so bad. Family at Christmas is a gift. The way it's supposed to be."

"I suppose every family has a crowd at Christmas."

"If they're lucky, they do. And if they don't, they get invited over." His father smiled above the neat rails they were replacing, the lengths of fir smelling faintly of fresh white paint. "It's been a long while since I've seen Rachel and the *Kinner*. I think the last time they were here was when your sisters were fourteen."

"Don't remind me."

His father chuckled. "Malena put a strand or two of gray in your mother's hair that year, all right. Little Susanna was only a year younger, but she'd hightail it into the woods when she saw your sister coming."

"Hopefully that won't happen this time."

"Malena has more important things to think about now than convincing her cousins to ride bareback when she thought no one was looking." He fell silent while Zach hammered the rail into place, then picked up the next and positioned it. "Must be strange for you, all your brothers and sisters getting married—or thinking hard about it."

Trust Dat to notice. "I'm glad for them. But I'm beginning to wonder if Deborah will be grown up and courting before I find anyone."

"Trust in *Gott, mei Sohn*."

"I do. I'm trying to be patient." He hammered the rail into place. "But if the twins decide to do some matchmaking for me, I don't know what I'll do. Last week I would have said *run away to New Mexico*, but now I guess it'll have to be Colorado. At least Onkel David and Aendi Leona will have work for me."

"Guaranteed. They're always short until the summer hands come back, or a trainload of Amish kids arrive."

Youngie from back East often came to the Amish community around the town of Amity to help on the ranches for the summer. Dat's brother David and his wife had four children, too, the opposite of Marlon and Rachel—three girls and a boy, plus two they'd adopted.

"I hope you won't leave, though, son," Dat said, positioning the next rail for him. "We need you here."

"Even if I get married?" Since he and his brothers were all partners in the Circle M, he meant it as a joke, but Dat didn't seem to take it that way.

"There's always that parcel of land on the point past Daniel's. It ain't as pretty as Adam's, but it's got good drainage, solid soils, and a nice view. Won't take much to extend the lane over to it."

Zach put down his hammer. "You'd allow me that parcel for a home? The one with the copse of aspens?" They turned gold in September, standing out among the more somber pines.

His father lowered the rail he was holding. "*Ja.* Daniel and Adam have theirs. Why shouldn't you have yours when the time comes? It takes all of us to work this place. Mamm and I aren't about to do anything that would make you pack up and move." As if to illustrate, he hefted the rail once more. "Unless you do the unexpected, like marry a girl from Canada or something."

"Not likely." There were only a few Amish communities in Canada—in Aylesbury, Ontario and on Prince Edward Island. It was unlikely to the point of impossible that he'd meet anyone from there other than his own relatives next week. When he got his breath back from his father's offer, he hammered the rail in and then moved to the next section. "*Denki*, Dat. I'm grateful. Though no need to get exercised about it yet. No point in building a home without a wife to live in it with me."

"One step at a time," his father agreed. Then, apropos of nothing, he said, "I expect Ruby will stay for supper."

"After all her help, the least we can do is feed her."

Two rails later, his father spoke again. "You'll take her home in the buggy?"

Zach's thumb nearly got a pounding. He focused on his work. "She usually walks. Except for last night. Dave Yoder drove her home."

"How'd that go?"

Zach shrugged. "I haven't had much chance to talk to her. They're busy making up the beds at Daniel's."

"So both brothers have had a try." Dat made a sound that might have been a chuckle. "I'd have thought one would be enough."

"It'd take a special woman to allow Calvin a second chance, I'll admit," Zach said. "But Dave's all right. Marriage will probably change his notions about what's proper and what's not."

"A grown woman might not take kindly to having to live up to standards outside of Scripture and the *Ordnung*," Dat mused. They were nearly done repairing the pens on this side. "Usually works better when she's living up to her own. Some things are better agreed on between a person and God."

Zach glanced at him curiously. "Are you talking about Ruby?" He couldn't think of anyone whose behavior would please God more.

"I'm talking about anyone. Worst thing a person can do is marry someone and expect to change them. You want to love the person who is, not who you think they should be, *nix?*"

That was true. "Unless you're Rebecca, falling in love with Andrew at first sight, with no idea about who he really was."

"That was a close call. Your mamm and I spent a lot of time on our knees about it. *Der Herr* was looking out for her, for sure and certain. And there was Noah, right there to hand, real as life."

"Real as life," Zach echoed as they finished up and collected the tools. He could say that about Ruby, at least. She was real as life—what you saw was what you got, with her. No pretending or trying to be something she wasn't, like Kate Weaver's awful sister.

For the first time, he wondered if Ruby was in the same boat as he—looking at the marriage prospects in the valley and not feeling that spark of attraction or possibility with any of them. The Stolzfus sisters, Beth and Julie, were fun and interesting and even pretty, and most everyone enjoyed being with them. But Zach couldn't see himself courting either one with serious intent. One of Dave and Calvin's sisters? They were neck-deep in all the doings of the *Youngie*, but only Sallie seemed to be the thoughtful type—when she stood still for two seconds. Besides, if he courted her, he'd have the prospect of Calvin for a brother-in-law, and that was enough to take her out of the running. Clara or Patricia King? He'd come to know them better because of Rebecca's marrying their brother, what with all the preparations for the wedding next week. They were as busy as his own mother and sisters. He could see himself as a happy and cordial in-law, but nothing more.

With a sigh, he put up his tools and followed Dat out into

the all too brief winter day. He'd take Ruby home. And maybe they could commiserate with each other about their marital prospects. It was the kind of thing he used to talk about with Adam, but his brother was wrapped up in Kate now. Which was reasonable. At least he could groan a little to Ruby. She'd groaned to him about Calvin asking for a date, and they'd had a *gut* laugh over how hard she'd had to work at convincing him the answer was *no* when he kept hearing *maybe*.

What would he do without a chum like Ruby? They could be singles together. Watch each other's backs.

But somehow this thought wasn't as comforting as it used to be.

&.

SOMEDAY RUBY HOPED SHE'D HAVE AS GOOD A COMMAND OF her kitchen as Naomi Miller. As they took their places at the table, there was no sign of today's baking—two hundred shortbread cookies iced in Rebecca's wedding colors of eggshell blue and lavender, with "Rebecca & Noah" piped on top by hand in white. All of them were safely between layers of waxed paper in airtight containers in the pantry.

Naomi had a special recipe box that held all her Christmas recipes, all neatly written on cards, some rippled and stained from her mother-in-law's Christmas dinners fifty years ago. Ruby knew that whenever the twins and Sara and Kate had a moment to spare, they had been copying out the recipes for the day when their turn came to host dinners for the family in their own homes.

Tonight's feast had come from the special box as a kind of working experiment for much larger meals when the New

Mexico and East Coast families arrived. A pork chop casserole made with onion soup gravy, dotted with red and green chile pieces sent from New Mexico. A coleslaw salad with green cabbage and red bell pepper, and a simple dressing that was scrumptious. Roasted sweet potato and Brussels sprouts drizzled with oil and balsamic vinegar. And not least, a Christmas salad made of red, green, and white layers of Jell-o and pineapple.

Adam gave Kate a glance when their silent grace had been offered and people had loaded their plates. Ruby saw her nod, and a happy thrill darted through her.

"Mamm, Dat, everybody," he began, "I want you all to know that this morning during our walk, I proposed to Kate ... and she said yes."

Pandemonium broke out as his siblings leaped to their feet to hug and congratulate the couple. Ruby couldn't keep the big smile from her face—nearly as big as Reuben and Naomi's. If this wasn't the merriest Christmas ever!

"Of course Kate said yes," Ruby leaned over to murmur when Zach sat down again beside her. "She's been in love with him for years."

"Doesn't do to take it for granted, though," he murmured back. "I'm surprised he didn't write her a letter."

"Too risky, as they've already proved. Where do they go on their walks?"

"Up to the meadow. If imagination had hammer and nails, Adam would have their place built already."

What a delightful image. "Have you drawn it for them?"

He laid down his knife to stare at her. He looked almost shocked. "No."

She hurried on, "Don't you and Adam talk about it? Wouldn't that be a *wunderbaar* wedding gift—one of your own sketches of their future home? You could even have it framed in town."

Behind that wide brown gaze, she could see the wheels begin to turn. "I never thought of it. Not even once. But you're right."

"Even if the house doesn't turn out to look exactly like the drawing, it would be like—like a moment marked in time. 'At this point in Adam's and Kate's courtship, their dream looked like this,'" she said, mimicking the auctioneer's patter.

His gaze came out of the land of imagination to the present, to the table, and he picked up his knife once more. "Thanks, Ruby. It's a really *gut* idea."

Warm with his praise, she returned to her own supper, and did her best to join in the conversation. At home, it was only Mamm and Dat and herself now. Being at a table full of Millers was a bit overwhelming, but if she spoke with Zach and the people sitting closest to her, she could manage it. What she was going to do when entire branches of the Miller family arrived, she didn't know.

Then again, there probably wouldn't be room here for folks other than the expected families. She was over here so much, always on alert for Zach's comings and goings under her busyness, that she needed to remember she wasn't a Miller herself. She was the bishop's daughter.

She sighed, and helped herself to some more sweet potatoes.

As if she could ever forget.

RUBY TALKED ZACH OUT OF HITCHING UP THE BUGGY TO take her the short distance home. "It's warming up," she said. "The thermometer says it's only twelve below. We'll be fine."

"You just don't want Hester getting chilly," he teased her as they set off down the lane. They wore winter coats, scarves, mittens, and boots. Zach wore a navy knit cap pulled down over his ears.

"Poor Hester only has her coat to keep her warm," Ruby said. "You're right, I don't have the heart to drag her out of the barn."

"I hope it doesn't warm up too much," he said. Each of them walked in one of the ruts the buggies had made. "We want the ice to be hard for the skating frolic on Friday."

The skating frolic. In all the excitement, she'd forgotten. "Who all is coming?"

"Nearly everybody. Plus any cousins who might have turned up by then. The ones from the East Coast phoned to say they'd got as far as Philadelphia, so they ought to be here tomorrow or Thursday. They might even be on the same train as Aendi Rachel and her family for the last leg."

It was quite a trip to make in the winter. "Canada to Chicago to Denver, and who knows how much snow in between."

"But we all travel in the winter. As the *Englisch* say, have wedding, will travel."

She had to laugh. "They do not." Spring, summer, and autumn were too busy for a large-scale event like a wedding, which the entire *Gmee* attended. Nobody could leave crops and animals to travel then. But in the winter, relatives traveled from all over the continent to celebrate with the young couple, renewing family ties and keeping old friendships fresh and alive.

"I don't want to shock you too much, but I'm looking forward to it," he confided. "I like skating. We'll have to watch that a hockey game doesn't break out."

"We *Maedscher* won't let it. Except Julie Stolzfus. She'd be right in there with you boys."

"You're a pretty good skater."

"We've all had lots of practice," she reminded him. "The hockey players have had more, though. Who gets to sweep the snow off the big bend?"

"Me, probably. Wish I had one of those blowers."

"And scare all the cows?"

"I know," he said, pretending to be glum. "Skates and a push broom it is."

"Friday morning I'll come and help you."

"You don't have to do that. Adam will."

"He's got a lot on his mind, and besides, he'll be with Kate. I want to. I like skating, too. It's a quiet sport that doesn't need a whole team."

"Which neither of us will ever admit to the Yoders. All right. You can have the new push broom and I'll use the old one from the barn," he said, generous in his capitulation. The push broom was easier to operate—you just skated back and forth, pushing the snow, at this altitude dry and light as laundry flakes, under the banks.

They emerged from the lane into the Wengerd yard, where the house lamps laid squares of gold over the snow. The walk had seemed to take only a minute.

"*Guder nacht*, Zach. *Denki* for walking me back."

"Never a problem. *Guder nacht*."

He vanished into the darkness, the sound of the snow squeaking under his boots fading through the trees.

Later, in her room upstairs, lying in the darkness under her quilts, she rewrote those moments so that they ended in a completely different way, with a kiss so sweet her knees trembled. At the age of twenty-two, she had never been kissed, so she had no idea what it was actually like. None of the boys in the valley had dared to try it—nor had she let them think there was even a possibility.

She knew one thing for sure and certain. She wasn't about to let anyone kiss her before Zach did.

MOUNTAIN HOME, MT

CIRCLE M RANCH
Monday, December 13

DEAR RACHEL,

We got your letter this morning, so I'm writing back tonight in hopes it'll reach you before you leave. Please telephone when you know which train you're on. My cousins from Prince Edward Island, Lorne and Salome Kuepfer and their family, are on their way too, and we amuse ourselves wondering if you'll all be on the same train to Libby. In any case, the big English taxi-van is on standby to pick you up, so be sure to let us know.

We have so much to talk about! But since you asked specifically about possible things you might do to keep body and soul together, I'm going to answer in the same spirit.

First of all, you're to be in no hurry about setting up housekeeping. You're welcome to stay here on the ranch as long as you like until you find a place to call home and work you enjoy.

Second of all, there are some possibilities along that line.

The Bitterroot Dutch Café is becoming more popular, and Ellie Bontrager was mentioning she might need another cook to help her come spring, especially if her daughter announces an engagement. Ellie is a dear woman and a faithful servant of God, but she takes some getting used to. So that's one.

Two, there's an old inn that's been standing empty in Mountain Home, where the creek crosses under the main road at the end of the downtown part. It's not for sale, but you might be able to rent it and fix it up. Reuben says the town needs more tourist accommodation, and there are plenty of hands to help. We want tourists and hunters and fishermen and skiers to stay and enjoy spending their money here instead of in Whitefish.

Last, we just heard that Marina Valdez, the housekeeper/cook up at the Rocking Diamond, has given her sixty days' notice. The Madisons are good neighbors—or at least, Reuben knows how to manage them so that they are. I don't know what they're like to work for, but you might talk to Marina and find out. You'd have to interview with Taylor Madison, I suppose. Bring along a treat—she likes things made of sticks and grass, or close enough.

We're so happy you're moving back to the Siksika we can hardly stand it. The kids will find a couple dozen young folk to make friends with—it will probably seem like quite a crowd compared to the Ventana Valley. And I'm looking forward to your coming for completely selfish reasons—nobody makes a wedding cake like you do, and Rebecca is beside herself with the hope you might make hers. No pressure!

I must close, and get this in the mail tomorrow.

With much love in Him,

Naomi and Reuben

. . .

P.S. AUNT RACHEL, THIS IS REBECCA, GETTING IN THE LAST word. I would love it if Susanna would be one of my supporters on the 21st. Malena will be the other, of course. Will you ask her? And if she says yes, we'll start making her a blue dress. She can finish it when she gets here. See you soon! Much love—R.

❦

Thursday, December 16

AT SIX-THIRTY IN THE MORNING, ADAM WAS THE FIRST TO hear the *Englisch* taxi-van's big engine coming along the neatly plowed highway, but it was only because he'd been haunting the barn door since they'd come out to do chores before breakfast. The train arrived in Libby at five, but with the snow, the trip had probably been a little slower than Jimmy, the driver, expected.

"They're here!" he called. "Just in time for breakfast."

Zach and their father finished feeding the horses and cows, buttoned everything up, and headed outside as a vehicle he'd never seen before rolled to a stop in the yard. It was like a short bus, but even then, he would not have believed that so many people could pour out of it.

Jimmy waved as he helped people down. "Had to bring the Boss," he called. "Fourteen people plus luggage was too much for the van."

Mamm ran out on the deck, wrapped in a black knitted shawl. "You did all come on the same train!" she cried. "*Kumm, kumm*, you're just in time for breakfast. Jimmy, you're welcome to stay, too, after your early start."

"Thank you, Miz Miller. I believe I will."

In the darkness before a winter dawn, Zach could hardly

tell one person from another in the crowd, even with the help of the house lights. So he and Adam made themselves useful on the edges of the melee, carrying luggage up to the deck as Jimmy hauled it out of the storage compartment under the bus.

There was a lot of luggage. They left it under the covered part of the veranda by the front door to be sorted out later, and went around to the basement door to take off their muck boots. Upstairs, he and Adam waded into the chaos of the kitchen, where three families were all talking at once.

Aendi Rachel enveloped him in a hug. "Look at you, all grown and strong. I'm happy to see you, Zach."

"So am I," said his cousin Tobias, at twenty-eight the eldest of Rachel's children. He corraled his seven-year-old twins just long enough to introduce them as Gracie and Benny, before they wriggled free and galloped away. Laughing, Zach shook hands, then Gideon and Seth, who were closest to him and Adam in age, grabbed him like the *Englisch* cowboys did, one hand shaking, the other clapping him on the back.

"Is this Susanna?" Adam asked incredulously.

The curvy young woman grinned, her eyes a sparkling blue and hair as black as a raven's wing under her bucket-shaped white *Kapp*. "Can't stay thirteen forever. You're still a tall drink of water, both of you."

Her hug was swift and nearly forced the breath from Zach's lungs. That's what ranch work would do for you.

"Remember my cousins from the Maritimes, Rachel? The last time you saw them was probably at Reuben's and my wedding." Mamm glowed with happiness that her guests had arrived safely under her roof. "Lorne and Salome Kuepfer and their family—the boys are Caleb, Jacob, and Aaron, that's

Emily there talking to Rebecca, and the younger girl by two years is Jenny."

Another round of greetings as Mamm's cousins caught up to date with Dat's family. Zach saw that Caleb was standing off to the side, as if this many relatives were too much for him as well. He sidled over. "There's a quiz on everyone's names before you get any dessert."

Caleb laughed. "At least the New Mexico folks have seen you all fairly often over the years. How does your mamm remember all of us?"

"Circle letters," Zach said wisely.

"Ah. I should have known. Mamm shares them with us, but it's been so long since I saw any of you that I forgot which of your sisters was Malena and which was Rebecca."

"You'll remember after a couple of minutes with them, trust me. Give me a hand with the table, Caleb?"

"Call me Cale."

Zach had brought out the eight-foot folding table and set it up at the end of the kitchen table last night when they'd heard from Aendi Rachel, but with the additional arrivals, they needed more folding chairs from the basement. The bench wagon was still in the barn from Sunday, but its use was reserved for the wedding, not for a family breakfast. When everyone was seated and they had said a silent grace, Mamm and Aendi Rachel and Aendi Salome brought in breakfast.

Roundup breakfast, to mark this special occasion—Zach's favorite of all. He liked just about anything in the food department, but there was nothing like fluffy biscuits and sausage gravy, with mounds of sausages to go with it, along with russet potatoes and sweet potatoes fried together in a cast-iron skillet with onions and sun-dried tomatoes, and jars of Aendi Rachel's hot chile salsa to spoon on top.

"It tastes like home," groaned Tobias blissfully. "I was never so hungry in my life."

"Travel does that to you," cousin Lorne said, digging in. "Ask me how I know."

"What is this spicy stuff?" little Benny demanded suspiciously. "I think it burned my tongue."

"You'll get used to it," Malena said with a grin. "Some people put ketchup on everything. We put Aendi Rachel's Hatch chile salsa on everything. Try the green version," she advised the boy. "It's milder."

"I brought a box of each color for you, Naomi. My Christmas gift," Aendi Rachel said to Mamm. "I don't know what we'll do next year—Montana's not quite the climate for growing chile. I s'pose I could have it shipped from my favorite farm instead of waiting for them to roll into the supermarket parking lot in Chama and set up the roasting barrels."

The Kuepfers looked mystified.

"The chile farmers bring burlap bags of chile in trucks from Hatch, New Mexico," Susanna explained. "They only come once a year, and you have to keep an eye out."

"Or follow your nose," her mother added. "They roast them in twenty-gallon drums and you can smell them all the way down to the Toltec railyard. There's nothing like it."

"Except maybe for a lobster boil on the beach, with corn and potatoes steamed in the pot with the lobster," Emily said, looking as though it was an effort to speak up in such a crowd, but determined to hold up the eastern end of the family traditions.

"Or Mamm's elk stew after roundup," Adam said loyally, "with baked potatoes and beans and tomatoes from the garden."

"We've had hands tell us they'd sign on to the Circle M just because of the feed after roundup," Rachel said, nodding.

"Go on with you." Mamm's cheeks were pink. "Who needs another biscuit?"

The morning was a bustle of getting everyone settled in. Cale, at least, was not only a light packer, but was fine with a blow-up mattress on the floor of the one bedroom at Daniel's house that didn't have a bed in it yet.

"I'll be breaking ground for my own house come spring," Adam said apologetically. "When you come next time you'll have your choice."

"Next time might be your wedding," Zach said, elbowing him. "Who wants a houseful of company on your wedding night?"

Adam blushed scarlet and escaped, leaving Zach and Cale to exchange grins.

"My brother's brand-new fiancée is Kate Weaver, who has my youngest brother Joshua's room up at the big house. Josh is married now and lives on his wife's hay farm," Zach explained.

"Your brother's fiancée lives with you?" Cale's voice was incredulous. "What do the *Gmee* think about that?"

He shrugged. "I don't know. Sara lived here, too, before she married Josh. Mostly as nanny for Nathan, but studying to keep her EMT license current, and working on her hay farm. Kate's home has been in Whinburg Township up until she and Adam came back in August. Didn't make much sense for her to be on the other side of the country when there's plenty of room here on the ranch."

"People have long distance relationships all the time," Cale said, not quite arguing. Zach wondered if he was hearing the voice of experience.

He gave a rueful chuckle. "Well, that got in the way for

those two. They're not taking any chances now—and besides, it's a lot easier to plan a house when your intended is across the table, not across the country."

"I guess so."

After thanking Lovina, who was baking a chocolate cake to take up to the house later for supper, he and Cale tromped up the lane, widening the ruts of the buggy wheels in the snow. His companion looked through the trees out over the river meadows, where the snow glowed in the winter sunlight, blue shadows reaching down to the frozen gray surface of the river. The wind pushed the skiff of snow hither and yon in snaking ripples, as though mimicking the movement of the water hidden beneath.

"Good skating down there?"

Zach nodded. "It's about seven inches thick. Tomorrow we'll sweep it off and have a skating frolic in the afternoon. To welcome you all."

Cale's nose and his grin were practically all Zach could see, sandwiched between his woollen scarf and the knitted cap pulled down over his ears. "Is that right, eh? Mighty neighborly of you."

He sounded so Canadian that Zach had to smile, too. "Any excuse for fun around here. And with you folks, we have enough for two hockey teams." Of course they would play hockey on Prince Edward Island—most of the Amish had come there from Ontario. "What do you play? I'm left wing."

"Center," Cale said.

No surprise there. He was probably captain, too.

"Can you ride?"

His cousin looked puzzled. "Ride what?"

"Horses."

The puzzlement turned to shock. "Of course not. Horses are for work, not leisure."

"Around here, horses are for work, too. Adam, Dat, and I sure appreciate extra hands when we ride fence, especially after a blow. We've always got posts falling over. Have to keep an eye on them. Don't want the cattle getting out."

"I guess not. I'd be happy to help, and I know Jake and Aaron would be, too." He crunched through the snow in silence for a moment. "So who is coming to the skating frolic? How many *Youngie* are in the valley?"

"A couple dozen," Zach said. "We're not exactly Lancaster County. I was out there one summer and there was a massive day out in Intercourse. Hundreds of *Youngie* and young couples and kids in this big park. Half a dozen volleyball nets all going at once, and people waiting to sub in. I'd never seen anything like it."

"I sure haven't," Cale agreed. "We have a couple dozen *Youngie* in our district, too. Probably the most on the Island."

"It's about the same here. We have two districts."

"So ... are you seeing anyone?"

Zach wasn't used to young men asking personal questions, but then, Cale was family. And if he went out East, Zach would probably be the one asking the same questions. "Not me," he answered easily.

"There sure has been a lot of courting in your family. Which I only know because Mamm reads Naomi's letters aloud when she gets them."

"I'd say there must be something in the water, except ours comes from a spring up on the mountain. We know exactly what's in it."

Cale laughed. "Our family is the opposite. *Gott* hasn't shown me or my brothers the woman He means for us. Or my sisters either. Though Emily was seeing someone pretty seriously, I thought—until he married a girl from away and went to live in Aylmer."

"Well, the whole bunch will be here tomorrow. Maybe *Gott* has just been waiting for you folks to come for Christmas."

"Maybe He has." Cale grinned again. "Maybe the girl of my dreams is hunting her skates out of the closet right now."

They'd reached the barn. "How about a lesson in tacking up a horse for riding?"

❄️ 4 ❄️

Friday, December 17

IN THE MORNING, having located her white figure skates at the back of her closet, Ruby put on two pairs of socks inside her thermal boots with the thick insoles and warm fluffy lining. Out on the frozen river at these temperatures, you didn't feel the cold in your feet until it was too late to do anything about it, and she was determined that cold feet would not spoil today.

Skates hanging over her shoulder by their laces, she walked over to the Circle M. When she reached the kitchen door, she could hear the racket all the way through the thick log walls. A happy Christmas racket—the sound of people visiting and laughing, of dishes being washed, of cousins catching up after many years apart. But before she could take off a glove and knock, the door swung open.

"Hey," Zach said with a smile. "I thought that was you passing the window. We've got a few extra hands here to make some light work. *Kumm*."

Being the only stranger in a roomful of people she didn't know made her even more shy than usual. But Zach was the same way, and he looked so comfortable with this huge crowd of family that she waded in and did her best to remember everyone's names. A couple of the boys began to put on coats and mittens.

"Honest, Ruby, if you want to stay inside with the girls, it's okay," Zach said, pulling on his knit cap. "We can sweep the ice."

"I didn't wear my thermal boots to stay inside," she protested. "Besides, I like to skate, remember?"

"So do I," said the tall young man with hair the brownish-red of a glossy chestnut. The oldest of the easterners. Cale, that was his name. "Makes a job easy if it's on skates."

"Maybe not if you're mucking out the calving pen," she pointed out, and he laughed.

"*Ja*, you're right." He tossed a pair of black hockey skates over his shoulder. "Let's do this."

Push brooms and house brooms in hand, they made their way down to the river, where it slowed in a deep bend. This was where they swam in summer, and was the part that froze first in winter. A couple of logs lay up on the shallow bank for purposes of removing boots and lacing skates, and before long, Ruby was stepping sideways down the short slope to the ice.

The first skate of the season—her legs and ankles remembering the balance, her face turning red with the wind of her movement—the long glide, the singing sound her blades made as she made a series of crossovers at the end and skated back. There was nothing like it.

Zach grinned as he stretched his legs, too, those long legs that made short work of the distance. In moments, he had joined her.

"It feels good, *nix?*"

"Perfect skating weather."

"All right, sweepers," he called. "Start up at the bend, in the middle, and sweep to the edges. Don't carry it all back again when you turn around—watch the wind. It'll try to undo your work."

Cale and his brothers watched her and Zach demonstrate, then pitched in. They soon found out that Montana mountain snow wasn't anything like the heavier, wetter stuff they got out East. It was like chasing waves and whirlwinds of soap flakes all over the river's surface.

Cale skated over after watching the wind carry his brother's broomful away and deposit it on his own nice, clean sweep. "How do you keep up with it?"

"Where's the wind coming from?" she asked, as though she were a schoolteacher quizzing a scholar.

He faced into it. "Northeast."

"So we start at the bend, like Zach said, where the smooth ice begins. You sweep with the wind, carrying the snow to whichever bank it would blow toward naturally. Usually the outward one. See?"

She skated away, the snow piling up in front of her push broom and then whirling obediently under the bank when she gave it a nudge.

"Smart," he said, doing exactly as she said with a much more successful sweep.

"Experienced," she retorted. "If we want to skate, we have to sweep."

"And then it snows again and you start all over."

"Probably not before this afternoon, though."

With so many helpers, the ice was cleared in no time, giving the boys a chance to stack wood scraps and branches from Adam's woodlot for a bonfire well in advance, instead of during the frolic itself. Overlooking the bend, Zach stood in the little meadow, likewise cleared of snow compliments of the wind.

Ruby told the guests, "We'll use the logs as benches, and have hot chocolate and snacks if we're not skating."

"Sounds like what we do," Jacob said, stacking the kindling in a neat teepee shape. "Usually at night, though, if it's cloudy and warms up a bit."

"Not too warm here at night in December, I bet," his brother Aaron predicted.

"Neh," Ruby said with a laugh. "There's a reason we do this in the afternoon."

At lunch, those who were sleeping at Daniel's trooped down the narrow road to eat. All except Cale, who somehow hadn't gotten Lovina's message. All through lunch he teased Susanna about something silly, but she didn't seem to mind. Afterward, Ruby sliced raisin pie into eight neat pieces, plated them, and put a dollop of whipped cream and a pie fork on each.

"Are you eating all those?" Cale asked, appearing at her side.

"Ha ha. Make yourself useful and carry these out to the living room, will you?"

She half expected him to make some smart remark about women's work, but to her surprise, all he said was, *"Ja,* sure," and put himself in the position of servant to his family.

It was nice to see. Unexpected. But then, why was she expecting him to be like Calvin Yoder just because he seemed popular and good at sports? They were nothing alike, except they were both tall and the eldest sons in their families. She knew better than to judge people—mostly because she found that people tended to judge her.

Cale came back empty-handed in a few minutes. "Better cut another one. There's a lot of people out there who like raisin pie."

She nodded. "I do, too. Make sure you save a slice for yourself."

"Back at you."

When everyone had a slice of pie, he ambled back into the kitchen for the slice she had waiting on the counter. She meant to join everyone in the living room, but he didn't seem inclined to. Instead, he leaned a hip on the counter and began to eat his pie. She leaned her backside on the warm door of the stove and picked up her own.

"I don't remember seeing you yesterday when we arrived, Ruby," he said. "I'm not related to you, am I?"

She had to smile. "I don't think so. I live on the ranch across the highway. Have done my whole life."

He nodded wisely, his pie already half gone, while she'd only taken the first bite of hers. The pastry was so good it was a crime to rush it.

"That's why you know all about sweeping ice," he said. "Do you curl?"

"Curl what? My hair? Of course not."

"*Neh*, curling, the sport. You know, where you try to throw a stone down the length of the ice and get it into the other guy's house—a circle drawn on the ice. To make it go where you want, you sweep the ice in front of it as it travels."

Come to think of it, she had heard of something like that. "I've never seen it. People in Canada must have a lot of time on their hands."

He laughed. "More like a lot of stones and ice. You make

do with what you have. It's fun, though most people do it in a curling rink, not outside."

"Hockey is easier, sounds like."

"No brooms," he agreed. "Except beforehand, like we did today."

She dared to smile. But he didn't see it, because Malena came in to get another piece of pie for her father, and Cale wandered back to the lively conversation in the living room.

Ruby understood. She couldn't be considered lively by any stretch of the imagination, and after all, he'd come all this way to see his family, not the neighbors.

She looked up to see Malena gazing at her. "The pie is *gut*," Ruby said. "Did you make this one?"

"I think you did—remember, on Tuesday when we made raisin and snitz?" She paused. "What do you think of Caleb?"

Ruby lifted a shoulder. "He seems nice. Many men wouldn't have carried the pie around."

"Zach would have. And Daniel." Malena darted a glance at her. "I hope Cale got a piece, too."

"I saved him one."

Malena waited a beat, then said, "How nice of you."

Ruby rolled her eyes. "Stop that."

"Well, it was. And why shouldn't you? He's nice, he's good-looking, and he's related to us. What more could a *Maedsche* ask?"

He's not Zach. And since she couldn't very well say that to his sister, she merely smiled and turned away to run hot water into the sink. The dessert plates wouldn't wash themselves.

Not long after, buggies and *Youngie* on foot began coming up the lane. As Ruby hung up the dishcloth to dry, she saw the Yoder family buggy roll in with Calvin at the reins, which meant that all five of the Yoder siblings were inside. That pretty much indicated that the frolic could begin.

"People are starting to arrive," she said to Zach in passing. "I'm going down."

"Me too. I'll just get the lighter for the bonfire."

Malena and Rebecca had already found skates and socks for all the cousins who wanted them—some of the skates were probably as old as Reuben, with something of his leathery endurance about them. The chattering herd put on coats and winter gear, and flowed down the steps and on to the river path on the far side of the barn.

Ruby smiled to herself. This was how a frolic should be—lots of visiting back and forth, anticipation of a good time, with a hot bonfire at one end of the trail and a warm house at the other. And for herself, well, anywhere Zach was meant a good time.

Zach lit the bonfire as people laced up their skates. Some of them decided that the bonfire was better than skating at keeping them warm—people like Simeon King and Susan Bontrager. Ruby shook her head and turned her back on them as she reached the ice and took her first long stroke. Thank goodness Simeon had never shown any interest in her. Imagine looking forward to married life with someone who behaved like a fifty-year-old instead of someone who wasn't even thirty.

Julie Stolzfus skated up beside her. "Could have predicted that," she said in a low tone, glancing back at the occupants of the log on the bank as her strokes synced with Ruby's. "Say, any chance of hockey?"

"I don't think so," Ruby said. "If there was, I'm sure someone would have brought sticks and a puck."

"I did." Julie paused. "But if you say so. Maybe it's not quite right to play shinny when the Millers have guests."

Ruby didn't understand her reasoning. "I don't know about being right. It's probably more that their company didn't bring their equipment all the way across the country. You know, in place of the wedding gifts."

Julie laughed. "I'll just leave my stuff in the buggy, then. The ice looks great!"

And she skated away, far more confident than Ruby could be. Where Ruby enjoyed the sound and the feel of the ice, the sense of freedom it lent her, Julie turned the glassy surface into a partner. No bubble or hidden rock would ever dare spoil that confidence, that unconscious dominance. In sheer happiness, Julie dug in one pick, flung out her hands, and popped into the air in a waltz jump.

"Show-off!" Dave hollered, a big fake grin on his face that didn't fool Ruby one bit.

"She's not," she contradicted him, skating past gracefully. "She's just happy to be on the ice."

But Dave, evidently, hadn't gotten over Ruby's turning him down for a second date. He didn't deign to reply, simply followed Calvin down to the second bend, their sisters in their wake like so many ducklings in black wool coats.

"What's gotten into him?" Zach asked as he skated up and matched her strokes. "Julie can outskate anybody here. Everybody knows that, like they know a chinook arch means a warmup."

"It's a mystery," Ruby said. "I think he's mad at me."

"Uh-oh." Zach grinned. "Turned him down for a date, did you?"

"How did you know?" A bolt of anxiety hit her. "Not a date, but a second ride home. Did he say something to you?"

He touched her arm, just enough for her to feel it through his mitten and her coat and sweater. "*Neh*, don't worry. Haven't you ever noticed Dave's pattern? He asks, a girl says *neh, denki*, he ignores her. I don't think he understands the concept of giving and taking offense. But by next church Sunday, he'll have thought it over and set his sights on someone else. Guess I'd better warn my cousins."

Ruby had to go a bit faster to keep up with his long strokes. "I had not noticed Dave's pattern. If I had a hundred years, I would not have noticed it. Because Dave Yoder is my brother in Christ and I try not to notice him at all." She eyed him, skating along without a care in the world. "Do I have a pattern?"

There was that grin, which meant a laugh might not be far behind.

"Not that I've seen. It's not like I'm hiding behind trees, watching you."

"I wish you would." The words popped out of her mouth as suddenly as Julie jumping into her waltz turn.

And there was that big laugh, which lasted all the way down to the second bend. Zach whipped around so he was skating backward in front of her, as they headed back up to the bonfire. "Is that what you need, Ruby? A friend to save you when someone tries to ask you out?"

Ja, if you're that friend, she nearly said. But that would never do. Instead, she tilted her chin. "Only with the Yoders. I'd be willing to pay the going rate, when you're available."

That set him off again. Still laughing, he turned—his skate hit a stick frozen into the ice—his arms and legs flailed as he fought to stay upright.

Before she could slow her own flight or even react, she hit the same stick, lost her balance, and crashed into him with all the grace of a bag of oats chucked into a wagon.

☙ 5 ❧

ZACH HAD the presence of mind to catch Ruby and pull her into his chest, before he allowed their momentum to take them down. He landed on his back, but not hard. More like a roly-poly bug curling into a ball.

"Oof!" He'd always thought Ruby was a slender person, but the force of her fall pressed the breath out of his chest for a few seconds. When he got it back, he gasped, *"Bischt du okay?"*

"Ja," she panted. "Sorry."

Only Ruby would apologize for being saved from clocking her skull on a frozen river. He grinned up at her. "What for? I got underfoot, not you."

An answering grin spread across her face—a mix of mischief and delight. "A fine cushion you make, though. Very comfortable." Her brown eyes sparkled, and for the first time, he got a good look at how long her lashes were. And how beautifully arched her brows—like the feelers of a butterfly.

"Are you all right?" With a singing scrape of his skates on the ice, Caleb Kuepfer came to a stop beside them. "That was a spectacular fall. What did you hit?"

Ruby tried to get her knees under her, but had to negotiate Zach's long legs first. "I'm okay. I'm not sure about Zach—I landed on him."

Zach sat up and acted like a hitching post so that she could get to her feet. "I'm fine. I learned how to grab and roll in EMT training. There's a trick to it so you don't break anything."

"You'll have to teach me that trick," Cale said with admiration, hauling him up. "Before we go out riding fence and I fall off a horse. Ruby, whoops!"

Her feet went out from under her and Cale caught her before she went down.

"Sorry," she gasped, the second time in less than a minute.

"Maybe you'd better warm up by the fire," Cale said. "I think your extremities might be getting cold."

Why hadn't Zach seen that? He was the volunteer fireman who'd had a whole day's training on frostbite and hypothermia.

"I've only been out here for five minutes," she protested. "It was just a stupid piece of wood frozen in the ice. I'm fine."

"He's right, Ruby," Zach said. "A couple of minutes at the bonfire and maybe a hot drink wouldn't hurt."

"Come on." And before Zach could protest or offer, Cale had taken Ruby's gloved hand and skated away with her.

She looked back, as though she was afraid Zach might think her ungrateful for risking life and limb—well, limb, at least—without even a thank-you. An apology wasn't the same thing. But then Cale said something, and she looked up to answer, and they were lost in the crowd of other skaters.

Malena and Alden Stolzfus circled him once, holding hands, before they glided to a stop. "Are you all right?" Malena asked. "That looked ugly."

"It was this." He dug his blade into the piece of wood

frozen in the ice, chipping it to bits and wishing he had some water to fill the hole with. And maybe working off some of the spurt of irritation at Cale's highhandedness with a girl he hardly knew. He skated to the bank and collected a double handful of snow, then tamped it into the hole. The slivers would blow away soon enough.

"Cale sure is nice," Malena went on, oblivious to the fact that her special friend was standing right there. "His sisters are, too. Emily told me they skate a lot at home."

"Their bishop frowns on hockey," Alden added, "but he hasn't put a stop to it yet, she says."

Zach did not care whether a bishop on the other side of the country frowned on the *Youngie*'s activities or didn't. "I guess Julie had better steer clear of Cale, then. She'll have him out here playing shinny before you know it." He dusted off his backside. "I'm going to do a few laps and warm up. Coming?"

But he soon left them behind, because it was nearly impossible to get up any speed when you were holding hands and whispering sweet nothings to someone.

It took half a dozen circuits around their makeshift rink before his feelings sorted themselves out and he was calm again. It had been stupid to get mad about another guy being nice to Ruby. She deserved to be treated well by every man in the valley. Zach was only angry with himself that he hadn't offered first.

He was practically her best friend—the one she turned to when a crowd got to her, because all too often crowds got to him, too. They'd find a quiet corner and didn't even have to speak. They just kept each other company until one or the other felt up to going back. He'd steal her favorite pastry— butter tarts—if they happened to be on offer at a singing or a wedding and sneak it onto her plate. And she always made sure he got a piece first of whatever she was handing around.

They looked out for each other. Because they were friends.

Except for just now. He'd caught her before she hurt herself, true, but it shouldn't have been a stranger looking out for her after that. It should have been Zach.

Which made him irritated all over again.

He'd just go check that she was all right, and maybe have a cup of cocoa himself.

His blades sang on the ice as he skated up to the landing, which was a grassy little point that had no big rocks to dull their blades. He went up sideways and found his skate guards stuck in the shallow drift where he'd left them. A plastic forest of skate guards had sprouted the length of the drift. But when he got to the bonfire, he couldn't see Ruby or Cale.

Rebecca was pouring cocoa out of a Thermos flask, and handed him a cup. "I thought Ruby was up here," he said.

"She was. Cale just took her up to the house."

A shiver of alarm went through him. "Why? She didn't hit her head—I caught her as she went down."

"Oh, is that what happened? No, she's fine." His sister shrugged. "Just maybe done with skating."

He looked up to check the weather. The sun was still above the ridge, but it didn't look very convinced about shedding any warmth. The clouds, however, had that peculiar smooth consistency that they got when the wind changed to come out of the west and a chinook arch was about to form.

"Noah's having way too much fun. Look, he's waving me out there, too," Rebecca said, waving back. "Can you spell me?"

"Sure." Zach figured he might as well pour cocoa for people. He and his siblings were hosting this frolic, after all.

Never let it be said that the Circle M wasn't hospitable, or that it might leave anybody out in the cold.

❧

HONESTLY, WHAT WAS A PERSON SUPPOSED TO DO IN THIS situation?

Caleb Kuepfer was being so nice, so attentive to her well-being, that Ruby couldn't very well drop his arm, turn around, and go back to the river. That would be ungracious, and if there was one thing the bishop's daughter should never be, it was ungracious. She often found herself saying *ja* when she wanted to say *neh*, of going when she wanted to stay, of agreeing when she wanted to debate. And it wasn't even her parents who put her in this position—or not often, anyway. *Obey thy father and mother* wasn't something you could debate. It was other people. Even the *Youngie*. Sometimes it was only because she agreed to go somewhere or do something that a frolic happened at all. As though people thought her presence gave everybody else permission to be there, too.

Which was quite a burden to carry.

Maybe that was why she liked it on the Circle M. Here, the family understood her. The most anybody asked her to do was help in the kitchen, which was where she likely would have been anyway. She liked cooking. Taking familiar ingredients and making something different out of them—the sum being more than its parts, *nix*? She liked looking after Rebecca's chickens the way she looked after her own. And she loved helping Malena piece a quilt once the latter had done all the hard work of designing it, choosing the fabrics, and cutting the sometimes complicated pieces. Sewing quarter-inch seams was easy, and the result was far more than the sum of its parts.

So the fact that she had to change out of her skates and tromp up the path beside Cale when she didn't want to was just plain irritating. But she would never show it. When a person was being kind, the last thing Ruby would ever do was discourage them in their kindness.

They found the living room full of parents—the Miller connections, mostly, but also Mamm and Dat. Ruby caught the surprise in her father's eyes when she appeared in the doorway with her hand tucked into a stranger's elbow.

She untucked it in a hurry.

"Bishop, this is our son, Caleb," Lorne Kuepfer said. Then, to Cale, "Back already?"

Cale shook hands with Ruby's father. "Ruby took a fall. It seemed she might need more than the bonfire to warm up a bit."

Ruby shrugged out of her coat because it was plenty warm in the room. The thermometer's needle on the woodstove stood in the orange zone.

"A fall?" Mamm said, looking her over carefully. "*Bischt du okay*, Ruby?"

Just what Zach had said. *"Ja, Mamm."*

"She fell on Zach and flattened him," Cale said with a grin. "Hit something in the ice that none of us noticed when we were sweeping it."

What Ruby noticed now was that people's pie plates and *kaffee* cups were empty, so there was only one thing to do. She hung up her coat and began to collect them. But her strategy to escape being the center of attention backfired when Cale started collecting the ones on the other side of the room. Before long they met in the middle and he walked out to the kitchen with her.

She just *knew* that Mamm and Naomi were having a silent conversation with their eyes.

Which she would completely ignore.

"*Denki*, Caleb," she said, piling the plates neatly next to the sink. She turned on the hot water and squirted in some dish soap. "You should go back outside and have fun. No need to stay in here."

"I go by Cale. And I am having fun." He snagged the nearest dish towel and leaned a hip on the counter.

Ach, neh. "Truly, it won't take a minute to do these. And you don't want to miss out on the hockey game if they get one going. Every player matters around here, because there aren't so many *Youngie* to make up sides."

"Trying to get rid of me?"

Oh, dear. She couldn't let him think that. "Of course not. But this may be your only chance to skate, with the wedding only four days away. And then Christmas, and church, and maybe you won't be staying so long after that—"

He laughed and took a plate from the drain rack. "Tell you what. Let's get these done and go back down together. With your hands in that hot water you'll be warmed up in no time."

It was half a victory. He might not have let her wash the dishes in peace, but at least she could go back down to the river. Where Zach was. Hopefully wondering what was going on when Cale didn't return, either.

"Did you walk over here?" Cale asked.

"When—earlier? Before we swept the ice? *Ja*, of course. My parents brought the buggy, though. Why?" She rinsed several plates at once and stacked them neatly in the drain rack.

"Oh, I just wondered if you'd go home with them."

"I expect so. It's not very far, and there's a full moon, but still. Dat will keep Mamm out of the cold if he can."

"Too cold for me to walk you home?"

The mug she was washing nearly did a somersault in her hands. Luckily she caught it. "I—well, I—" She stumbled to a halt while a hot blush rose in her face.

She didn't blush like a pretty rose, the way Malena did. Hers was more like a heat wave, from the chest right up to the roots of her hair. If she went outside and put her face in a snowdrift, she'd melt a hole in it.

"I know I only met you a few hours ago." His voice was gentle. Maybe he thought the hot water was causing her red face. "But our time here is short, and..." Self-assured Cale Kuepfer didn't seem to know what to say next. "I don't want to embarrass you."

All right, he knew it wasn't the hot water. He knew he was making her blush. Never mind a snowdrift, she was about to melt a hole in the kitchen floor.

"Maybe ... you already have a special friend and I'm horning in where I don't belong." He waited a moment. She couldn't have answered to save her life, but she had to tell the truth.

She shook her head.

If her heart could have wailed in distress, it would have. But it just went on beating, pumping blood into her face and making her want to run away and hide.

"I'm amazed," he confessed quietly. The pie plates made soft clinking sounds as he stacked them. "A girl as pretty as you, always willing to help, who can skate like the wind? What are the men in the Siksika thinking?"

Unbidden, a smile trembled on her lips and faded.

"I saw that," he said. "Maybe I'm not such a klutz at this after all."

She dared to flick a glance at him. "You're not a klutz." *I am.* She let the water out and scrubbed the sink as the suds swirled around it. But she appreciated his humility. For a young man who was so good-looking and confident, how could he not have a special friend himself? "I'm sure the girls on Prince Edward Island don't think so."

"You'd have to ask my sister." His rueful smile held none of the self-satisfaction of a man claiming his popularity with the girls in his district. It was almost as if he really didn't know what they thought of him. "I just had a pretty big breakup. For sure and certain not one girl in either of the Maryfield church districts will touch me with a fishing gaff."

Ruby found herself wanting to know why not. But she couldn't ask him. Nor could she ask his sister without sparking a firestorm of gossip and speculation, and that was the last thing she'd ever do. She hadn't wanted to know he was free, either, but he'd told her openly.

He was so nice. What had happened to cause such a big breakup?

Never mind. She didn't want to know. Because his freedom or lack of it had nothing to do with her.

"But," he went on in a low tone, "I'd sure like it if you'd let me walk you home. Give me something happy to remember about my trip to Montana."

Maybe the girl had dumped him flat and taken up with somebody else. He was hurting, she could see that now. It wouldn't be dangerous to say yes, because his heart was full of that other girl still, and probably would be for months.

And while Zach would have walked her home without hesitation, it was a simple fact that he would do it as a friend. And that would make her cry herself to sleep again, because Zach was never, ever going to see her as anything more. None of the other young men in the Siksika held a candle to him, and it was plain she couldn't have him. So why not walk home with Cale?

It wouldn't mean anything to Cale, and for once maybe she could fall asleep with someone else on her mind.

"All right." She wrung out the dishcloth and hung it up. "I'll walk home with you. But for now, let's get some skating in before the sun gets any lower."

His smile could have lit up a room.

At least he had the good sense to douse it before they went into the mud room and collected their coats. She didn't want to give her mother any more ideas.

❧ 6 ❧

MALENA AND ALDEN took a turn at serving hot chocolate, which meant Zach was free to get back on the ice. He wasn't in the mood to hang out with the *Maedscher* by the bonfire. He was just taking off his skate guards when he saw Cale and Ruby up by the house, coming down the stairs and clearly heading back to the frolic.

He didn't know what impulse made him slip the guards back on and stump over to the woodpile to throw another couple of chunks on the flames. Or to join in the Yoder girls' chatter and reply to their eager questions that he was just fine after his fall and so was Ruby.

"I bet she is," Sallie said with a giggle. "Nothing like falling for someone—literally—to make him take notice."

He was about to correct her—*he* had cushioned Ruby's fall —but bit back the words just in time. Because the fact was that all these girls could see was Cale. Zach wasn't the kind that girls seemed to notice. Not like Daniel, or Josh. Adam was about halfway between the two extremes. So he smiled at the joke and poked at the fire with a little more force than necessary.

All it took to put the blues berries in his glum muffin was to see Ruby and Cale skate off together, their strokes falling into a rhythm so naturally that Sallie gave her sister Maryanne an *I told you so* nod.

Get a grip. She's your friend and he's your cousin. There is nothing wrong with them skating together.

It was just a skate. Harmless fun. Though he couldn't remember a time when Ruby had actually made a preference for anybody known quite so publicly. She wasn't that kind of person. If she did go out with someone, none of the *Youngie* knew about it until after the fact, and only then if the man of the hour talked about it. That was rare, because the teasing he'd get about cozying up to the bishop was more than most could take for very long.

Cale would escape the teasing because he was from away. In any case, after Christmas the Kuepfers would leave and everything would go back to normal.

For Zach, that day couldn't come soon enough.

It wasn't so bad at supper, with everyone packed into the house eating off plates in their laps wherever they could find a place to sit. No one in her right mind would cuddle up to a young man in front of her parents and his if they weren't engaged. Some couples wouldn't do that even if they *were* engaged, and their parents would find out there was going to be a wedding when the bishop announced it in church.

Still, it seemed every time Zach got a look at Ruby, Cale was passing by, or leaning over to say a word, or offering her something as he took a plate to where he was sitting.

Fine. He'd just stop looking.

Which meant he saw Sallie elbowing Malena with a meaningful glance at the other end of the room.

Good grief. Did Ruby have any idea what people were beginning to think?

After supper, the first stars were pricking out in the sky when the buggies began to roll down the lane, people hollering *guder nacht* and *denki* out the doors. Little Joe Wengerd collected Sadie at the bottom of the steps and called a good-natured thanks to Zach as the horse started down the lane. It took Zach a second to realize that Ruby wasn't with her parents.

With a lightening of his spirits, he loped up the steps and found her in the kitchen with Malena, Rebecca, and Susanna, talking and laughing just like every other time she came over. The Kuepfer *Youngie* were out in the living room telling their parents all about how much fun they'd had, with his cousins from New Mexico having to admit that while it got plenty cold on the ranch, they didn't have freezes like they did here.

Everything had returned to normal already. Something that had been coiled tight in his chest gave a great sigh of relief and relaxed.

"I'll check the barn," he told Dat quietly on his way out. "You stay and enjoy yourself."

It looked like Dat hadn't moved out of his chair since baby Deborah had fallen asleep on his chest. Deborah would be the kind of baby who was used to lots of people around, talking and eating and making a bunch of noise. She was probably going to be like Malena, who loved company and frolics and activity.

Zach headed for the peace of the barn, where the cows didn't expect him to converse, and the horses nodded at his approach. He made sure everyone had feed and clean hay, and saw that the animals recovering from injury in the calving pens were quiet and comfortable. Zach buttoned up the shop and tack room, took the lantern off its hook, closed the door firmly against the cold, and walked back up to the house.

The dishes were done, and there was no sign of Ruby. She was probably getting her coat on, waiting until he came back to see her home. He slipped out the kitchen door and walked around on the deck to the front, intending to intercept her, only to stop so suddenly his boots skidded on the thin layer of frost forming on the planks.

Ruby was the last to leave, as usual. Except for the family still talking and visiting in the living room.

Except for Cale, who was not talking and visiting, but walking beside her out of the yard. They strolled under the shadows of the pines on either side of the lane, the sound of their quiet conversation fading into the winter silence.

Zach didn't know how many minutes passed while he stood there, frozen in surprise and dismay. It was as though time had stopped. As though he were waiting for it to start up again— over again—with Ruby coming out the door and him joining her, and the two of them ambling up the lane together, the snow crunching under their boots.

But nothing changed except that he got colder.

Until he finally realized what he was doing.

He was waiting for Cale to come back. Timing how long it usually took. Wondering why it was taking him so much longer than it took Zach to make the same familiar walk.

You idiot. Go to bed and stop embarrassing yourself.

Because honestly, even if Cale did come back in the next minute, what was Zach going to say? *Are your intentions honorable toward the bishop's daughter?* Cale would laugh himself sick, and he'd be right to do so. It was none of Zach's business who

Ruby skated with or walked home with or accepted a buggy ride with.

They were just friends.

He should be glad that a nice guy had taken notice. That she had smiled more tonight than he'd seen in a while. That her parents had met him and hadn't found anything to object to.

Everything was fine. It was all fine.

Which was why Zach forced himself to go inside and down into the basement, where he stoked up the woodstove for the night. And if, when everyone had gone to bed, he happened to be standing by the window of the bedroom he shared with Adam, keeping an eye on the lane to Daniel's house in the light of the full moon, there was no harm in it.

"Are you still awake?" Adam's voice was groggy as he pushed himself up on one elbow. "What are you looking at? Is there a bear?"

Zach shook his head. Cale had just appeared below, hands in his coat pockets, walking with an easy stride down the lane to his own bed at Daniel's.

"Just making sure all our company finds their way to bed." He indicated the lane with his chin. "Cale just came back."

"From where?" Adam flopped back on his pillow.

"He walked Ruby home."

"I thought you did." His brother yawned and turned over.

It took Zach a minute to paw through what he wanted to say versus what it was fitting to say to Adam, who knew him better than anyone. But by the time he'd arranged the words, Adam had gone back to sleep.

Monday, December 20

THE PREVIOUS FRIDAY NIGHT, RACHEL MILLER HAD succumbed to Rebecca's pleading to apply her considerable skills to her wedding cake. So on Saturday, Rachel had commandeered the kitchen, her sister-in-law, and both Susanna and Malena to help create the most important cake of the bride's life. It also meant that the bride was chased out of the kitchen to make her final decisions about the bridal table in the *Eck*.

In their own kitchens, Ruby already knew, her mother, as well as Lovina Wengerd Lapp Miller and Sara Fischer Miller, were all making snowball cakes, thick with coconut-flake frosting, for the wedding table in the *Eck*, but the wedding cake would have its own table. Under it would be a square white cloth embroidered all around the edges with bachelor buttons and glacier lilies to signify Noah and Rebecca, and sprigs of lavender—the *spikenard* spoken of in Scripture—to signify purity and devotion. Malena had designed it, and Ruby and Rebecca had finished the embroidery on Tuesday, just before all the Circle M family arrived.

Malena's plans for a host of cupcakes, half frosted in eggshell blue and the other half in lavender and arranged on tiered cupcake stands, had to be put off until today. This, in Ruby's mind, was cutting it a *little* too close to a Tuesday wedding. But cupcakes had to be fresh, and the wedding cake took priority, so all of Saturday had been devoted to it. Yesterday had been the off Sunday in the western district, but not even Malena would dream of baking on the Lord's day, no matter how fast time was running out.

Ruby emerged from the Circle M lane just as the sun peeked through the gap in the mountains, turning the snow-covered fields and paddocks to glowing white. She had long ago given up trying to stop her gaze from rambling over the view every time she came over, hoping for a glimpse of Zach. In the distance, moving among the darker bodies of the cattle wintering over closer to the home paddocks, were two horsemen and a man driving the hay wagon. She recognized Zach at the reins of the wagon, but couldn't make out his features—only the forward tilt of his hat and his broad shoulders under the heavy coat. One horseman moved with the assurance of a born rancher—Gideon, the second of Rachel's three sons. And the other ... Well, that had to be Cale or one of his brothers, riding the cutting horse as though it were a bronc and he expected to be bucked off at any second.

Smiling, Ruby climbed the steps up to the house, let herself in, and braced herself for the onslaught of noise and activity. Every room seemed to be a whirlwind, from Reuben, Daniel, and Seth, the youngest of Rachel's sons, setting up the benches in the living room for the service, to the racket of female voices and the clash of dishes in the kitchen, to the sounds of cleaning from upstairs.

"Ruby, thank goodness," Salome Kuepfer said breathlessly, catching sight of her standing in the kitchen doorway. "We've just cut the cake for the favors, and Joel is here to help you wrap them."

"The table belongs to us, Ruby," the boy said. "Mammi said so."

Up to her elbows in dishes, Naomi smiled over her shoulder at her grandson. "Everything is ready. Wrap each piece, roll it in a doily, and tie it with that thin ribbon in each color."

"Even if it's women's work," Joel finished as Ruby seated herself.

Naomi made a rude noise that made him grin in delight. "Wedding work is everyone's work."

Reuben leaned in the kitchen doorway. "I wrapped cake for favors when Mammi's sister Julia got married," he told Joel. "That's how Mammi and I fell in love."

Joel shot a horrified glance at Ruby, and she burst out laughing. "Don't worry, Joel, history is not going to repeat itself. Let's get to work."

Poor Joel learned in no time the sneaky habits of cling wrap. So Ruby took over that part while he rolled each piece in a small, round paper doily, then stacked them. When they were all done, he held each piece while she snipped lengths of blue and lavender ribbon and tied them in a bow around the little bundle.

It was finicky, fussy, sometimes maddening work, but by ten o'clock it was finished. And nobody would complain if she and Joel ate the broken pieces left over from the applesauce spice cake, rich with raisins and chunks of apple. It had caramel frosting in the middle to contrast with the rolled almond frosting on the outside. Rebecca fetched the basket she'd been saving. She'd already lined it with a smaller cloth she'd clearly embroidered herself to match the one that would go under the wedding cake.

"It's beautiful," Ruby said in admiration as they laid the pieces carefully in the square basket.

"That's the only way I'm like my twin," Rebecca said with her dimpled smile. "Both of us like to make things beautiful if we possibly can."

"A wedding is a particularly *gut* day for that," Ruby agreed. She didn't add—because it would embarrass modest Rebecca —that the bride was the most beautiful of all. The girl who could disappear in plain sight, who kept social events in motion while being nearly invisible herself, had blossomed in the sunshine of Noah's love.

The sparkle in her eyes and the joy and anticipation in her face when she looked at him had made of her a woman who drew the eye. And the eyes of everyone around her were filled with love.

Ruby went into the big living room to get her first look at the *Eck*. Rebecca had laid the tables with robin's egg blue tablecloths, then with lavender napkins and her new china at each place setting. It looked lovely. Naomi's silverware and Kate King's glassware rounded it out.

"Tomorrow when we put up the tables for the lunch," Rebecca said, "we have Mason jars with raffia bows filled with baby's breath. Some of those will go here."

The thump of boots came from the mud room, and a tingle passed through Ruby as Zach, Gideon, and Cale trooped into the kitchen.

"Thermometer's rising with this west wind," Zach said to Rebecca with a smile. "We'll likely get a white Christmas, but I wouldn't be surprised if it's above freezing for tomorrow."

"I sure hope so," Gideon put in. "I've never seen anything like this chinook wind. How is everyone holding up in here?"

He shouldn't have asked. Naomi was ready with a to-do list for each of them. "But first we'll have coffee and cowboy cake," she announced.

"I don't know about you, but I feel like I've put in a whole day already," Cale confessed, coming over as Ruby hastily cleared the kitchen table of ribbon and stray paper doilies. "What's cowboy cake?"

"It's like a coffee cake, with spices in the mixture and a crumb topping," she said.

"What have you been up to?"

"Making favors," Joel told him. "Me and Ruby wrapped a couple hundred pieces of cake. It's good." He patted his stomach. "Really good."

"My reputation is preserved," Rachel said, straight-faced, from the stove, where she was taking the cowboy cake out of the oven.

Cale laughed. "Let's hope some of the cake was, too."

"Oh, it is," Rebecca said, lifting her basket to show him. Then she took it down to the basement, where Ruby knew an entire shelving unit was set aside for wedding food—so much that she wondered the shelves didn't bend in the middle.

Since only a dozen or so could sit at the kitchen table, and the benches filled the living room, Ruby and most of the *Youngie* ate their cake and drank their coffee standing up. Zach collected his plate and joined Ruby at the far counter, where Naomi normally rolled out her pie pastry.

"Somehow I don't remember Joshua's wedding being quite this crazy," he murmured.

"You have a lot more company staying at the ranch," Ruby pointed out from behind her coffee cup. Sara had had no surviving family, so it was only the church and the Millers. "They're staying for Christmas, *ja?*"

"That's the plan. What about your house?"

"My brothers and their families are local, of course, but they're all coming for Christmas dinner and staying over for church, and my Aendi Rosemary is coming from St Ignatius for the week. She'll be here by Thursday. Mamm is so happy. Mind you, the *Kinner* will be sleeping on air mattresses in my sisters' old rooms. But I don't think they'll mind."

"That'll make two of us hiding in the barn," Zach said.

"*Neh*, it's different when it's your family. Don't you think so?"

He looked as though he might disagree, then finally said, "*Ja*, it is. Did you hear that Mamm is going to take Aendi Rachel out for a tour once things settle down?"

"A tour?" Ruby glanced at him curiously.

His gaze fell to her mouth. He tapped the side of his own, and she realized with a gulp she must have cake crumbs on her face. She wiped them off as his gaze settled on his aunt at the table.

"Of the valley. She's looking to settle here."

Ruby stared at him. How had she not heard this before? "Leave New Mexico? The whole family?"

"*Ja*, apparently they and the bishop's family are the last ones left on the Ventana River. When Aendi Rachel moves, the bishop has already told her he's taking his family back to where they're from. They've got *Kinner* of courting age, and his wife is all afire to get them into circulation, she says."

She had to laugh at Rachel's colorful way of looking at it. "My goodness. Well, they've come to the right place if the boys want to keep on cowboying. But what about Rachel herself? And Susanna?"

"Well, that's what the tour is for. They're going to drive around and look at the possibilities."

Ruby turned over some of those in her mind. "She could open a shop, like Rose Stolzfus."

He nodded. "Or go to work at the Bitterroot Dutch Café."

"Once Susan marries Simeon King, Ellie will need help," she agreed.

"Think that's a given?"

A glance around the room told her that everyone was occupied in conversation and *Kaffee*. "Can you keep a secret?"

"Nothing is a secret in this house." But his voice had dropped to a level that invited confidences. An intimate level.

She pulled herself together. "Sim came to see Dat the other night."

No more needed to be said. Zach nodded and looked wise. "It was only a matter of time. In fact, I'm surprised it hasn't happened long before this. Does Rebecca know?"

"I don't expect so. Not unless Sim told Noah."

"Then I'll keep it under my hat." He paused. "Speaking of secrets, did you have a nice walk home after the skating frolic?"

An odd feeling struck her, as though someone had tapped a bass drum in her stomach. "Not really a secret, but *ja*, it was nice enough. Short. Cold."

"I hope you invited him in to warm up before he came back."

What did he mean by *warm up*? She chose the most obvious. "I did, in fact." Carefully, she set her coffee mug on the counter. Her hands were shaking for no reason whatsoever, so to cover it, she addressed herself to her cake a little more seriously. "How did you know Cale walked me home?"

"I came out to offer, like usual, and saw the two of you heading down the lane."

He'd come out to offer. And she'd been hasty and accepted the first offer she'd received.

Neh, she corrected herself. *The person who wanted to walk you home, who didn't see it as usual, as a custom, as a duty even, is the one who walked you home. He didn't take his time getting around to asking. Didn't take you for granted.*

Zach seemed to be waiting for more information. And really, there was no reason not to give it.

"Mamm and Dat were still up, so we made tea and had a short visit."

"*We* the two of you, or *we* all four?"

"All four, of course. He wasn't there to court me, Zach."

"Don't be so sure. He's been hovering around you like the bees around Grossmammi's trees in blossom time."

Was that a compliment? Did he think she was like an apple blossom?

Neh. Not Zach, who was not given to flights of fancy or poetic language. That was Adam's department, from what Kate had said about his letters.

"You're imagining things," she told him. "He's just being nice. There's no point in anything else, if they're going back home in the New Year."

"Well, I'm glad you think so. He might think differently."

The zinging of the blood in her veins cooled as though snow had been added to it. "If he did, would it matter to you?"

Her whole being seemed to hang on his next words. Where on earth had she found the courage to just blurt it out like that, in a crowded, noisy room, with no thought beforehand? It might have been the bravest thing she'd ever done.

"It's none of my business, Ruby," he said.

As if she'd been released from a rope, she was falling through space, with no one to catch her. No one to care.

"No, I suppose not." She let her cake fork land on the plate with a tiny clang, picked up her empty mug, and walked away to get started on the dishes.

❧ 7 ❧

REBECCA AND NOAH'S WEDDING DAY

Tuesday, December 21

THERE HAD to be a hundred people packed into the Miller home—both the Siksika churches, as well as the family staying over and even a few guests visiting their own families in the district. Andrew King had returned from Whinburg Township, though Zach privately thought it was less for Noah's wedding than to publish it far and wide that Elizabeth Weaver, Kate's sister, had said *"Ja"* when he said, "Will you?"

Zach would never say it out loud, but Andrew's presence definitely had a flavor of "Look, Rebecca, I'm engaged to the most beautiful girl I've ever seen after you turned me down—and now you have to settle for my plain, responsible brother."

It would never occur to Andrew that Rebecca couldn't wait to marry plain and responsible Noah and leave the management of handsome and feckless Andrew to someone else. Nor would Andrew understand that to Rebecca, love made the man now standing at her side perfect, because she knew without a doubt that Gott had intended him for her.

"*. . . und glaust daß es vom Herren ist und durch dein glauben und gebet so weid gekommen bist?*" Little Joe asked her solemnly. *And do you believe that it is from the Lord and that you have come so far through your faith and prayer?*

"*Ja,*" Rebecca said softly, her eyes downcast in the solemnity of the moment.

Zach had learned to appreciate the simplicity of the vows an Amish man and woman made to each other—that they believed marriage to be ordained by God, that each believed God had provided the other for them, that if one needed help in sickness or adversity, the other would provide it. Then, lastly, came the words that changed a person's life: "Do you promise together that you will come with love, forbearance and patience to live with each other, and not part from each other until God separates you in death?"

Both Rebecca and Noah answered clearly, "*Ja.*"

A smile played about Little Joe's lips as he took Rebecca's right hand and quoted from the book of Tobit: "*And he takes the hand of the daughter and puts it in the hand of Tobias.*" He placed Rebecca's hand in Noah's right, then clasped his own huge paws around them.

"The God of Abraham, the God of Isaac, and the God of Jacob be with you together and give His rich blessing upon you and be merciful to you," he said in a voice that carried through the entire house, even to the bedroom where Sara was walking a fussy Nathan. "To this I wish you the blessings of God for a good beginning, and steadfast middle years, and your walk forward to a blessed end. This all in and through Jesus Christ. Amen."

He, Noah, and Rebecca bent their knees in reverence at the holy name.

"Go forth in the name of the Lord," the bishop boomed, the smile breaking free. "You are now man and wife."

Noah and Rebecca didn't have far to go forth—only back to the chairs set for them, with their *Neuwesitzern* on either side. Malena and Susanna supported Rebecca—slipping her a tissue to blot the tears of joy from her cheeks. Simeon and Andrew sat on either side of Noah, the former gazing straight ahead and the latter sneaking peeks all around the room, as though to catch people looking at him.

After a few words of testimony from the deacon and the ministers, Little Joe asked Reuben Miller if he would like to say a few words.

Dat stood, his mouth working with emotion as he gazed on his daughter and new son-in-law. "I wish you gentle rains and bright sunlight to walk in faith," he said hoarsely. "Storms and dry times to grow in faith. And an open home and a loving family to reward you in faith." He lifted his head to address all the guests. "Thank you all for coming—Naomi and I are glad for each one of you. I hope this day will be a blessing to you all as it is for us."

After a prayer as familiar to Zach as the *Loblied*, the wedding was concluded with a hymn.

> *Freu dich Zion du heil'ge G'mein*
> *Dein Bräutgam wird schier kommen,*
> *Der dich hat g'macht von Günden rein,*
> *Das Reich hat er schon g'nommen.*

> *Die Stadt die hat er schon bereit,*
> *Da du solt sicher wohnen,*
> *Er gibt dir auch ein neues Kleid,*
> *Von reiner Seiden schone.*

Rejoice, O Zion, thou holy church
Thy bridegroom is almost come
He who has purified thee from sin
Has already taken His kingdom.

The city He has made ready for thee
There thou shalt safely live
He gives thee also a new garment
Of pure and lovely silk.

The new clothes the bride and groom and their wedding party had made for this occasion, Zach thought, were the shadow, the forerunner, of that day when *Gott* would provide His church with new, pure garments, making them worthy to go in as a bride to the wedding supper of His Son.

When the hymn concluded, the bridal party stood in the *Eck* to receive the congratulations of friends and family, while Zach, Adam, and the other young men of the congregation got to work setting up tables for the wedding meal. The tables were barely on their feet when the young women came along with the white tablecloths from the bench wagon, acting in waves—cloths, plates, cups, and finally, a knife, fork, and spoon wrapped in a blue napkin tied in lavender ribbon laid across each plate.

There were so many—twice as many as a normal church Sunday—that Mamm had said they would eat in two settings. Zach and his siblings would eat in the first one with the bride and groom and their *Neuwesitzern*, as members of the immediate families, while Mamm and Dat and Arlon and Kate King joined the wedding party in the *Eck* for the second setting. After the silent grace, he couldn't help but notice that Ruby, too, was eating at the first setting, as a member of the bishop's family.

Normally he could catch her eye without an effort—they tended to share any given event with a smile or a lift of the fork with something particularly tasty on it. But not today. He could see her quite clearly near the window, eating her wedding roast—chicken and stuffing mixed together, which they both loved—as methodically as if it had been ordinary macaroni and cheese.

There was nothing like a wedding for an amazing feed, and he had to admit the Circle M rose to the occasion. Along with the must-haves, like roast and creamed celery, there were dishes peculiar to the Kootenai that couldn't be left out, like venison pot roast, and scalloped potatoes rich with cream. Zach liked cornbread salad, which started with broken-up cornbread and bacon and just got better from there. Adam was already on his second helping of Boston baked beans—made with barbecue sauce, of course—while beside him, Kate reached for the Christmas-style broccoli salad she'd made, where she'd added chopped red pepper and sunflower seeds to make it festive. Since Christmas was at the end of the week, Rebecca had to have one more nod to the traditional colors, with a three-layer jellied salad in green, red, and white, turned out on a doily with slender pine branches peeking out from underneath. Of course there were mountains of biscuits, slabs of butter, and as many kinds of pickles as there were vegetables in the garden.

Zach absolutely would not attempt to get Ruby's attention. While she was not one of the official helpers, who were usually young marrieds who hadn't yet started families, or members of the bride's buddy bunch, it was no surprise to see her rise from the bench and help with the clearing. And for the entirety of the second setting and even the visiting and festivities afterward, he no longer saw her in the crowd.

He didn't see Cale, either. That couldn't be *gut*.

For Rebecca's sake, he made the sacrifice of sociability, even though his whole being cried out for some peace and quiet, preferably with Ruby. There would be plenty of time for that after Christmas, when the Kuepfers headed home and the ranch settled once more into its low-key winter activity. But for now, he found himself making the rounds, talking with people, laughing at their jokes. And all the while, he looked for her.

Then he wished he hadn't.

For in the kitchen, a production line had formed for the dishes as they were carried there in stacks by the helpers. There was Ruby at one side of the double sink, and Sallie Yoder at the other, both up to their elbows in suds. Cale and Julie Stolzfus were drying on Ruby's side, with Kate Weaver and Calvin Yoder on Sallie's.

Of all the men he had never expected to find in the kitchen, these two would have headed up the list. There was nothing for it. Someone with some muscle had to take those heavy stacks of dishes out, and it looked like it was going to be Zach.

"We'll box them afterward," Kate reminded him as he took the first stack of plates. "Naomi says she'll use her own china for supper, since there won't be such a crowd."

"I don't think I can face supper," Cale groaned. "I'm so full that if someone tells me a joke, I'll burst instead of laughing."

With a superhuman effort, Zach resisted the urge to refer helpfully to Proverbs 23 and its warning about what happened to gluttons. Ruby might think he was acting more like a schoolmarm than a cousin.

So, as fast as the helpers dried the dishes, he stacked them ready to go back out. But Ruby and her team didn't seem inclined to take it easy. Instead of catching her in a hallway or a quiet corner to ask her how she was, Zach was forced to stay in the kitchen, being as bright and cheerful as he could, while the dishwashers leaned on the counter and waited for the dishes to return. Then it was all hands on deck until every last cup and spoon was boxed and he and Cale and Calvin had lugged them down to the bench wagon.

"One thing about sitting in the *Eck*," Calvin puffed as Zach closed and latched the doors of the big wagon, "you don't have to do the dishes. How do they handle this in places like Lancaster or Holmes County? There'd have to be a dozen dishwashers working hard to handle it all."

"And two or more settings," Zach said. In Whinburg Township, people had big equipment sheds, and barns, too, because the congregations were so much bigger than in the Siksika.

They climbed the stairs to take a breather on the deck, to find Andrew King out there taking a break from his duties as *Neuwesitzer*. "Dishes done?" he asked cheerfully.

Zach nodded.

"Elizabeth and I will probably have three or four times as many guests as this," he said, gazing at the number of buggies parked along the lane.

"When is the wedding?" Calvin asked.

"We're thinking Valentine's Day," Andrew said.

Cale's eyebrows rose. "A worldly holiday? Our bishop would question it. But hers doesn't, I guess."

Andrew grinned. "If he does, she'll talk him around. I don't care what the date is, as long as it's sooner rather than later. I want those vows said in front of the whole *Gmee* before she changes her mind."

Again. Elizabeth had been engaged at least three times that Zach knew of. But he'd never say something so unkind to Rebecca's new brother-in-law.

Cale lifted his face to the warm chinook wind blowing in from the west. "This feels *wunderbaar.* How often does it happen?"

"Maybe once a month, if we're lucky," Zach said. "It can last just long enough to make a mess before it freezes solid again. We have to be careful to get what doesn't melt shoveled out of the lane. Re-frozen slush will cut the horses' feet."

"Good weather for a walk," Cale said, apropos of nothing.

A walk with Ruby? Was he already planning to walk her home again? *Oh, no you don't.*

"Feel free," he said. "But as a member of the family, you ought to stick around to support Rebecca."

"Oh, I didn't mean *now*," Cale said, almost sounding shocked. "There are about fifty people in there I haven't met yet. Come on. They should be about ready to hand around the cake."

He was right. Noah and Rebecca were going from table to table as people finished dessert and drank their coffee, handing them favors and thanking each one for coming to celebrate with them. The snowball cakes had been demolished, and the cutting cake too. People were starting in on the iced short-bread cookies, which sounded like a great idea to Zach. If he had to visit and be sociable, at least it could be with short-bread in one hand and coffee in the other.

Ruby appeared at his side so suddenly he wondered how on earth he hadn't seen her, when he'd been scanning the room for her over people's shoulders for ten minutes. She took a bite of her shortbread. "Mm. It's a shame to eat something so pretty, but it sure tastes good."

"Rebecca will forgive you," he said, warmth spreading through him at this evidence that they might be back on their usual footing. "That was quite an operation you had organized in there."

"It needed to be organized," she said. She showed him the hand without the shortbread in it. "I have prune fingers. So does Sallie. The things we do for our friends."

"Nobody eating shortbread can be suffering *that* much," he told her with a grin. He was about to add more, when Cale popped up like the coyote you just couldn't get rid of.

"Who's suffering?" his cousin wanted to know. "Not you, Ruby?"

Wordlessly, she turned over one hand and showed him her prune fingers.

"A heavy price to pay," he said, nodding solemnly. "But think of it as laying up treasure for when it's your turn. People will be happy to do the dishes when you're the bride, won't they?"

The nerve of this guy! Zach nearly choked on the last bite of his shortbread.

"That's not why we help," Ruby managed to get out. A blush was already staining her cheeks, and she shifted from foot to foot as thought she wanted to be anywhere but here.

"Of course not. Many hands make light work, even if they're pruney." Cale captured her hand and turned it over to have a closer look, holding it as gently as if it were a rose. "Not so much now. You'll recover."

Ruby reclaimed her hand, completely red in the face.

"Careful," Zach said in a low tone that might have just missed being good-humored. "You're embarrassing her."

But Ruby was already gone, doing what the *Englisch* called a *fade* every bit as thoroughly as Rebecca ever had.

❧

CALE HAD AN EASY CONFIDENCE THAT IN SOME WAYS, RUBY would have liked to have herself. But he'd gone too far. Taking her hand like that and practically caressing it, right in front of Zach! Ruby had done her level best to be brave today—talking to folks in the other district whom she didn't see often, playing with the *Kinner*, even conversing with the Miller relatives, young or old, male or female.

But now she couldn't be brave. She just wanted to hide and find some restoration for her soul in solitude.

Ruby had been been to a worldly wedding once, hired by Taylor Madison along with the Miller twins and Sallie Yoder as a server at the Rocking Diamond. She'd seen the dining room table piled high with beautifully wrapped gifts that were like pieces of art in themselves. But such a show wasn't the Amish way. Instead, Rebecca and Noah would pay wedding calls on those who had come today, and at some point during the evening, a gift would be quietly given and gratefully received. Only those like Cale's family, who had come a long distance to be here, might have brought a gift with them. Still, it wouldn't be displayed. It would be in a bedroom, to be unwrapped and appreciated in privacy later.

She slipped into Rebecca's bedroom upstairs—which as of tonight, she'd share with her husband until spring breakup, when the ground would be soft enough to sink a foundation for a home. Ruby couldn't help a sigh of happiness and admiration, though, at the sight of the quilt already spread upon the new double bed.

Glacier Lily.

It had come just before Thanksgiving, and up until the moment Malena had given it to her twin, Ruby had been the only person in whom Malena had confided. In fact, Ruby had picked up the box addressed to Malena sitting next to the mailbox, put it in the buggy because of the rain, and taken it up to her one day when the family were all out. Malena had been stricken silent with astonishment as she'd opened the box and fished out the letter sitting on top.

Dear Malena,

You're probably pretty surprised to see this, but I figured who better to have it than the one who spent all that time making it?

You may have seen my ugly mug on a magazine in the grocery store after Ride Forever *came out. I suppose it's too much to hope that you might have gone to see the movie that I spent all that time preparing for at your place. But anyhow, it got great reviews and made so much money during its opening run that I was able to buy a house in Malibu. That's on the beach, out here in California.*

I also met a girl—one of the supporting actresses. You won't approve, but she moved in here, and sad to say, her taste in interior decorating isn't quite the same as mine. She's a genius, but homemade quilts, no matter how beautiful, don't fit into her ideas of the perfect home.

I could have sold it or auctioned it off for charity, but then I thought, well, you were pretty attached to it. And it does kind of belong in Montana. I asked my assistant to have it cleaned and so here it is.

I hope you enjoy having it back again, and maybe once in a while when you look at it, you'll think of me.

Your friend,

Cord McLean

"It's the perfect thing," Malena had breathed, folding up

the letter and pulling Glacier Lily in all its blue and golden glory from its waterproof box.

Ruby hadn't understood what she meant at the time, but she did now. For Rebecca loved that quilt almost as much as Malena did, and had never quite accepted its having to go to California with a man who had bought it in a spirit of competition, to spite another, not because he loved it. Now Rebecca and Noah would be able to enjoy it, keep warm under it, and cuddle their *Kinner* on it, for the rest of their lives.

A floorboard creaked, and Ruby turned. *Don't let it be*—

"I hope I'm not disturbing you," Emily Kuepfer said, hesitating just inside the door. "Rebecca said I might come up and see her wedding quilt."

"I had the same thought." Ruby walked around to the foot of the bed so that Emily could get the full effect. "This is the first time Malena appliquéd a flower wreath. Isn't it lovely?"

Emily sighed—the kind that indicated happy satisfaction. "What a beautiful quilt. Where did she get the pattern?"

"She designs them herself." When Emily's eyes widened, then she leaned in for a closer look at the piecing, Ruby went on, "She's got one hidden away called Montana Lupine—it would almost be worth getting married to have that one."

Emily straightened and huffed a breath like a silent laugh. "I'm sure it's only a matter of time. From what I hear, anyway."

Cool air from the window brushed across the back of Ruby's neck. "From what you hear?"

Emily tilted her head and exaggerated rolling her eyes in Ruby's direction. "I'm a bishop's granddaughter. Need I say more?"

"Oh, you poor thing," came out of Ruby's mouth before she could stop it.

Now a chuckle trickled from the other girl's throat,

discreetly, as though she were trying to keep it under wraps. As though it wasn't quite proper for the bishop's granddaughter to laugh out loud, right from her toes.

The way Ruby could remember laughing only a handful of times.

"I've been rumored to be engaged twice now. And when it might have been true—" She stopped, then went on in a voice with a protective veneer brushed over it, "My brother thinks very well of you."

How was she expected to reply to this?

"He enjoyed his walk home with you last night."

To be polite, she said, "I enjoyed it, too. He met my parents."

"So he said. He tells me the *Gmee* here call the bishop Little Joe. Is that because he's so tall?"

"*Ja*. The nickname was Daadi's doing, apparently, when Dat started growing as a boy and didn't seem to know when to stop."

"I can hardly imagine it." Was Emily thinking of her grandfather, the bishop? Who quite possibly didn't like the sound of a woman's laughter?

Ruby hoped the man never met Dat, then, who never failed to make Mamm laugh at least once a day.

"I wondered ..." Emily trailed off. "Or rather, Caleb wondered if you might let him drive you home from singing on Sunday. You have those here in winter, don't you?"

It was a moment before Ruby could speak. But she had already made up her mind, hadn't she? All her decision needed was a few words to make it real.

"*Ja*, just like everywhere. Church is at the Keim ranch. It shares a fence with your cousin Joshua and his wife Sara's hay farm, about five miles from here." The Keim place was one of the farthest out toward the hills—and five miles was a long time to be alone in a buggy with a young man. Maybe that was the reason Cale had picked this Sunday. But that was silly. How would he know where the Keims lived?

And she was prevaricating. Putting off the moment to speak. *Oh, come on. Cale is leaving. And it won't hurt Zach Miller to see that some people notice you in a special friend kind of way, even if he doesn't.* Besides, she'd already convinced herself that there could be no danger of Cale's feeling more for her than he did right now, so he wouldn't get his heart broken.

The thought of herself—Ruby the shy, Ruby the silent—breaking anybody's heart was enough to make her smile.

Unfortunately, Emily happened to turn her head just then and saw it. "Does that smile mean my brother can go ahead and borrow a buggy?"

"*Ja*, he can," she whispered, and it was done.

What was five miles between friends? And once it was over, Cale would be gone, and maybe Zach might not take her quite so much for granted.

As the *Englisch* might say, it was a win-win.

8

As the bride, it was Rebecca King's prerogative to match up the *Youngie* for supper as she saw fit, whether that meant a little bird telling her its preference, or her own tender heart having mercy on someone shy and pairing them up with a cousin, or knowing her own brother well enough to do the right thing. It did not occur to Zach that Rebecca would not partner him with Ruby. His sister knew better than anyone that he and Ruby were best friends, that he found her company soothing—and in fact, that he would rather sit next to Ruby saying nothing than put up with someone like Sallie Yoder, who was the most popular *Maedsche* in the district.

So it shocked him to the core when Simeon, as Noah's eldest *Neuewesitzer*, called his name along with that of his cousin Jenny Kuepfer, of all people, who was barely eighteen and hadn't been running around very long.

Jenny? Not Ruby? What was Rebecca thinking?

But there was no way he could embarrass poor Jenny, who blushed and could barely find her way out of the bedroom the girls had gathered in, or make her way with him down the staircase, even though she hung onto his hand in a death grip.

Who was Ruby going to eat supper with?

He managed to get himself seated across from Jenny just in time, for Simeon called Cale's name and Ruby's name and Zach froze in complete horror, staring as they descended the stairs hand in hand, Ruby blushing as Cale bent to say something private in her ear.

"Zachariah?" Jenny whispered. "Are you all right? You're almost as white as this tablecloth."

He heard her as though he were under water, the way he heard his siblings when they were all swimming and his ears were plugged up. And then the sense of her words finally penetrated, about the time Cale and Ruby sat down at the other end of the table.

"I'm fine," he said, and picked up the first thing at hand to offer it to her.

Jenny peered at him. "*Neh, denki*, I don't need a peppermint. Not before supper."

Surprised, he looked at the glass bowl of blue, lavender, and white mints. "Oh."

"*Bischt du okay*, Zach?"

"I'm fine," he said again, putting the bowl back in the middle of the long table.

To his relief, the helpers brought out supper. The *Youngie* had been singing for the last hour, songs that both Rebecca and Noah liked, as well as old-timey hymns and even one that Noah introduced as having been written by one of the *Youngie* who used to live in Colorado. Zach had already forgotten the name of it, but it was about walking a little while with Jesus, and letting Him guide you home.

Ruby's hand had nestled in Cale's as he escorted her down

the stairs.

And she'd seemed to like it. Not just permitting it out of custom, but accepting his hand because she wanted to hold it. Because she preferred Cale's hand to Zach's.

Who had asked Rebecca to pair them up? Cale, because he wanted to make a show of courting her in front of everyone? Or had Ruby claimed the privilege of friendship with Becca and done it quietly, unbeknownst to anyone?

He'd never held Ruby's hand that way. A piercing sense of loss shot through him, the way a stone thrown hard pierces the water, trailing bubbles behind it.

Of all the ways he'd taken her hand—to help her up after a fall on the ice, to guide her through a meadow riddled with gopher holes, to haul her off the sofa in fits of giggles at some stupid joke before she went home—he had never once held her hand the way Cale had just now. As though it were precious. New. Extraordinary.

Jenny handed him a jar of green salsa and he took it automatically, then realized the pan of enchiladas dripping in cheese had gone right past him. So he had to take his plate and get up to get some, trying not to look as though he was looking at Ruby.

She certainly wasn't looking at him. She was talking to Cale and smiling.

The salsa was hot, but he ate it and the enchiladas and the taco salad and everything else Jenny handed to him without registering much except that it tasted like sand. And when Malena's cupcakes came out on their tiered cake stands like so many Christmas trees set on each table, he took a deep breath and refused to let his stomach heave.

He simply smiled weakly at Jenny and mumbled an excuse about needing a minute.

of her at the skating frolic when it was *me* cushioning her fall, sitting next to her— Ach, Mamm, it makes me sick to think of it."

"You did look like you were going to lose your supper when you left the house."

"I almost did."

"But is Ruby the kind of woman to fall for a man like Cale?"

"What—good-looking, nice, capable? And a cabinetmaker to boot. He and Lorne have a pretty successful business, even if Lorne is too humble a man to say so. Cale was telling me about it when we were feeding the cattle the other day."

"And what is a good-looking, capable cabinetmaker doing in the Siksika with courting on his mind? Aren't there any girls on Prince Edward Island?"

He shrugged. "Maybe not right now. Jenny told me at supper she was glad to see him taking notice. His special friend broke up with him. All the girls are being a little stand-offish until they see whether he's going to get back together with her."

Which answered Naomi's question. "There you have it. He's had a breakup, his heart is hurting, and there's Ruby, the bishop's daughter. The perfect rebound girl to show that other girl he doesn't care. And if I know the Amish grapevine, this other girl will hear about it sooner or later."

Zach stared at her. "You're making that up."

Naomi had to laugh. "Maybe I am. But the fact remains that the Kuepfers are leaving right after Old Christmas. He can't be serious about courting Ruby when it's not likely he'll ever see her again."

"They are leaving then? For sure and certain?"

"That's what Salome tells me. Cabinets and dressers don't

make themselves, and they have orders to fill."

Zach straightened, as though something awful had occurred to him. "What if Cale stays?"

"You heard what I said about the orders? He wouldn't do that to his father."

"Maybe for Ruby, he would."

"Now *you're* making things up," she scolded him, in the most loving way possible. "The question is, how are you going to show Ruby you care for her, now that you know it yourself?"

"I—well, I—" He stopped. "I don't know what to do other than what I've always done. Be her friend."

Naomi let that soak in.

"That didn't get me anywhere, did it?" he said, as though answering himself. "I've got to do something different. But how, if Cale is always around?" He sat up straight. "I'll walk her home tonight. Get there ahead of him and ask her."

"And tell her how you feel?"

He shook his head, already getting to his feet. "She'd never believe me. She still thinks of me as a friend. I have to *show* her how special she is. What she means to me."

Naomi stood, too. She followed him into the bustle of the barn, of horses being led outside, of men bidding Reuben *guder nacht* and congratulating him on Rebecca's marriage and the establishment of another home in the valley where the Spirit would dwell.

As Zach went to help someone hitch up, Reuben saw her and lifted his brows in surprise. She'd tell him later, in the privacy of their own room. No matter what he said about her skills as a matchmaker, the two of them would do what they could for Zach and Ruby. Because Reuben, of all men in the world, knew how difficult it was for a silent man to speak up and say the words that could change a woman's life.

9

RUBY DEARLY LOVED A WEDDING, but by the end of a day that had begun at four o'clock in the morning, she was exhausted. Emily must have seen it, for she came over as Ruby was bracing herself for the next onslaught of dishes.

"Jenny and Susanna and I will finish up," Emily told her. "You look done in. There's no reason for you to stay ... except maybe one I could think of, and he's out in the barn."

She barely managed to bite back the words, "Zach is in the barn?" Because of course he would be, helping people hitch up and enjoying the company of the men—or, knowing Zach, the horses.

Belatedly, she realized Emily had to have meant her brother.

"*Denki*, Emily," she said. "I saw my parents go out a little while ago. I can probably still catch them."

"Are you sure? It's late. Cale will walk you home."

"I'll just go check." Which could mean anything—Mamm and Dat, Cale, Zach. She made her escape, but instead of turning left and going down the back steps to the barn, she turned right and climbed the path that led up to the meadow where Adam and Kate planned to build their home. Theirs, she mused, would probably be the next wedding on the Circle M.

The chinook wind had melted half the snow already, but a path that was clearly used a lot had been tramped through the drifts that remained. The waning moon still shed enough light to see by, especially in this world of white and black—a world she knew by heart.

By heart. What a strange expression that was, when usually, you knew something in your head, your mind. But some things you did know by heart.

Zach. Still living there in her heart, in the spot he had occupied since she'd been four years old and smitten, gazing up at his eight-year-old self. He'd been pointing out the flowers by the side of their lane after church and identifying each one for her as she picked it. She remembered them still—Queen Anne's lace, bachelor buttons, buttercups. From him she'd learned that when people talked about brown-eyed Susans, they didn't mean that bossy Bontrager girl, which is what she'd thought up until then.

"Ruby!" Snow crunched behind her, and she turned in surprise.

"I was hoping I'd catch you." Cale Kuepfer grinned and handed her a cake favor, still carefully wrapped. "You forgot this."

"What—my goodness—*denki*," she stammered. "But I already ate mine." She shoved it into her coat pocket.

"You have to have one to put under your pillow." He fell in beside her, considerately leaving the trampled path for her and widening the edges a little for himself. "How else will you dream about the one you're going to marry?"

She'd dreamed plenty of dreams about Zach. Wishful thinking.

"That's up to God, not a piece of cake," she said dryly. "Where are you going, so late?"

"I'm walking you home," he replied, as if this were a given. "At least, I think I am. Where are we going?"

She couldn't help but laugh, and pointed at the ridge. "This is a shortcut. You can see our house from there. But you don't have to, Cale. I've known the way since I was little."

"Maybe so, but I saw you head up the slope and it didn't feel right to let you walk through the woods alone."

Let her? "I do it all the time. The bears are all hibernating, so there's no danger."

"I'm less worried about bears than about my cousin Gideon, who was searching the house for you. I thought I'd better grab my opportunity and whisk you out from under his nose."

This was going too far. "Now, wait just a minute. Since when are you the one to *let* me or *whisk* me or anything else? I only just met you. All of you."

He pulled in his chin, as though her outburst had surprised him. "Well, I saw Gideon looking at you during 'O Blessed Hope.' There was this one line..." He sang, in a surprisingly nice tenor, *"The Bride shall hear the Bridegroom's voice; Look up, my heart, in Him rejoice.* But you didn't look up or hear Gideon singing, luckily for me."

Oh, honestly! "I was looking at the songbook, and not thinking of him *or* you."

You were thinking of Zach. Well, he was neither Cale nor Gideon, *nix?* She hadn't told a fib.

With a chuckle, he said, "Got you riled up, didn't I?"

"Not in a good way. Watch your step on this path. It's

bound to be slippery."

She took the opportunity to put a little distance between them. There was something to be said for the advantage of familiarity with every rock and runoff. When he caught up with her on top of the ridge, she pointed at the glow of lamplight between the pines in the distance. "That's our place. I'll be fine from here."

"I wouldn't feel right just leaving you out here, Ruby. This goes down to the highway, doesn't it?"

"It comes out right opposite our lane."

"I'm still coming with you."

With a spurt of wordless irritation, she turned and set off down the trail. But this was the dark side of the ridge, and the rock she usually used as a step was no longer frozen in place, but embedded in soil that had softened. It turned over under her boot. With a shriek, she went down, the fall made twice as far by the angle of the slope.

"Ugh!" Every bone in her body felt its impact on the hard ground, including her head. Freezing water seeped through the elbows of her coat sleeves, her dress, her tights. She had to get up.

"Ruby!" Cale exclaimed, sliding down and showering her in slush and mud. "What happened? Are you all right? Can you move?"

She couldn't get her legs under her. How humiliating. "Help."

He pulled her to her feet, and pain zinged up her left leg to detonate in her brain. She cried out and staggered, and he caught her. Then, as easily as if she were only a pillow, he swung her into his arms.

"Arms around my neck. You can navigate."

The tricky part had been the slope, now behind them. He

followed the well trodden path through the snow all the way to the road without the least bit of difficulty, then walked down their own lane with a long-legged stride that brought them to the kitchen door far sooner than she expected.

Or wanted.

Because there was Dat, halfway to the house from the barn, where he'd clearly just put up the horse. When he caught sight of them, any faint hope she might have had of getting into the bathroom unseen vanished like water on a hot stove.

"Ruby! Is that you? What has happened?"

"She took a fall on the shortcut, Bishop," Cale said cheerfully. "Can you get the door?"

Her father opened the kitchen door for them, and Cale went through with Ruby's feet first, so she wouldn't knock her injured ankle on the door jamb.

Mamm turned from the stove, her eyes wide.

Cale deposited her on a kitchen chair as though he'd been carrying young women around the countryside all his life. "There. You're all right now. Let's get these boots off and see what your ankle looks like."

"I'll see to her," Mamm said with a smile, moving in front of Ruby so gracefully that Cale fell back and, before he knew it, became the audience, not the participant. Mamm's strong fingers felt her ankle, and Ruby jumped practically off the chair with a howl.

"Wiggle your toes?"

Breathing hard from the pain, she did so.

"Not broken. But it's the ankle with the strained ligament from a couple of years ago. Got some swelling already." She glanced up at Dat. "It's been a while since the boys needed the liniment and a tension bandage, but I think they're still in the bathroom, under the sink."

Dat fetched them, and in minutes, Mamm had anointed and wrapped her ankle and propped it on a cushion on a second chair. Only then did Ruby realize that Dat had finished making the herb tea they liked to drink before bed, and a steaming cup already sat on the table next to her elbow. He'd even put milk in it, the way she liked. Cale had one, too. Mamm's pretty teacup looked as fragile in his big hands as Dat's did in his own.

"Bet you're glad I insisted on walking you home," Cale said with a grin that just missed being smug, but only because it was the truth.

She was glad. Sort of.

"If I hadn't been looking back to see if you were finding your footing, I wouldn't have fallen," she said crossly.

"Ruby..." Mamm said into her teacup.

She remembered her manners. "*Denki* for bringing me home. It isn't far, but it would have been difficult to hop on one foot the whole way."

"Is there a rag handy?" Cale scanned the floor. "I seem to have brought a bunch of mud and snow in."

Mamm found him one, and in a moment the kitchen floor was shiny clean. Not everyone would have thought to do that.

"So she strained a ligament before?" he asked Mamm while he rinsed the rag and hung it up. "Coming over that trail?"

"*Neh.*" Mamm glanced at her. "Coming into home plate, I think. It's been a while, but I suppose an injury like that leaves a weakness."

"That rock turned under my foot and I was down before I knew it. I couldn't stop myself."

"Ah well, a few days at home won't hurt," Dat said. "You've been over at the Millers' so much I thought they'd make up a bed for you."

"There was a lot of work to be done, and you both were over there just as much," she chided him with a smile. "Between the cleaning for church, cooking for the wedding, and getting rooms ready for Cale's family as well as Rachel Miller's, every pair of hands was welcome."

"I understand we're the first overnight guests that Daniel and Lovina have had," Cale said. "We'll try to leave it as neat as we found it."

"You're not heading out soon, though, are you?" Dat asked. "Someone was saying not until after Old Christmas."

Cale nodded. "It seems like a long time away, but with Christmas and church this week, our visit will be over before we know it."

"What is it like where you live?" Ruby felt as though she ought to keep up her end of the conversation. "Do you have as much snow?"

"We sure do. It's different, though. Heavier and harder to shovel, because we're right on the Atlantic and it's full of moisture. Our district is in the southwest of the Island, which on a map looks like it ought to be sheltered. But when a big nor'easter blows down from Newfoundland, the snow in our yard is just as high as it is on the north shore."

"You're a cabinetmaker, I understand," Dat said. "We have one or two of those here, too."

Cale said, "Dat and I have a shop in the barn, and my cousin is thinking of joining us as an apprentice. We make everything from bedsteads to cabinets to fancy front doors for *Englisch* folks, complete with carving and beveled glass."

"There's lots of work?" Ruby asked.

"*Ja*, people are beginning to discover there are Amish on Prince Edward Island, with a good reputation for woodworking. Just like they've discovered there are Amish here in

Montana, and in Colorado, and other places besides Holmes County or Lancaster County. At home, the tourists come for Anne of Green Gables and then they see my sister's quilts flying in the wind on the clothesline, or they see a little sign for a bed and breakfast inn at the end of a lane, and they discover us."

"We have an Amish-run quilt shop in town," Mamm said. "You've met Malena's special friend Alden? His mother owns it."

Ruby added, "Malena sells her quilts there. We're pretty spread out, and the lanes into the ranches are long sometimes, so even if she hung a quilt or two on a line no one would see it."

"*Ja*, I've noticed a few have cellphones, and are open about it," Cale said. "Is that because you are so spread out? Our bishop doesn't allow them."

"A few of the bishops out in the west had a chat about it," Dat said. "We use them for emergencies only. We've had a few occasions when a family gets stuck in the snow, or someone is out on the allotment to locate a lost calf, or an accident happens, and a cell phone is the only reason a person is alive today."

"Three out of four seasons here can kill you, my *grossdaadi* used to say," Mamm put in, her hands wrapped around her cup. "And the fourth one is thinking about it."

Cale laughed. "Our whole district is maybe the size of the Circle M and this ranch together. I can see where the distances would make it difficult to communicate any other way."

"Not too far to visit back and forth, though," Mamm said comfortably. "You're welcome to come by and see how Ruby is getting on, if you like."

A hot blush scalded Ruby's cheeks, and if she could have slid off her chair and under the kitchen table, she would have.

But Cale's gaze didn't move from Mamm's face. "*Denki*. I might do that. I hope she's on her feet again for Christmas. Do you have family coming?"

"*Ja*, Ruby's brothers and their families, and Joe's sister," Mamm told him. "The girls are too far away in the eastern part of the state, but their in-laws are closer, so their *Kinner* still get family time with their grandparents."

"Ruby is the youngest, then?" At last he looked at her. Ruby could only hope the blush had faded to something less than splotches of red. "The only unmarried child still at home?"

"*Ja*," Mamm said. "Until *der Herr* takes a hand in it."

Ruby swung her foot off the cushion. Enough was enough. "I'm going to bed."

Dat rose as she balanced on one foot, one hand clutching the table. "One of Daadi's canes is still in the closet. Let me get it for you."

Her grandfather had carved several of these before he died. This one was redwood, with a nice knot that formed the handle. With its help, she was able to hobble across the kitchen to the stairs. "*Denki* for bringing me home, Cale," she said over her shoulder. "*Guder nacht.*"

"*Guder nacht*, Ruby. See you soon."

She could hear conversation resume as she made her slow way up the stairs. Part of her wanted to stay, and hear about another church district whose ways and location were so different from their own. But she'd committed herself now, so she'd just go to bed before her parents made other pointed remarks that could only be construed as encouraging.

She'd go to bed, and do her best not to dream about Zach. That way only led to disappointment and tears.

𝕰 10 𝕰

Wednesday, December 22

THE DAY FOLLOWING a wedding was always cleanup day, and the bride and groom pitched in, too. First on the list of tasks was taking care of the bench wagon, so they'd finished loading benches early. Sara and Joshua came for breakfast, Sara and Nathan to help and Joshua to drive the heavy wagon over to the Keim place and bring the horses back.

Cows waited for no man, so Adam saddled up while Zach and Cale hitched one of the horses to the small wagon they used in the fields to take hay to the cattle. As Daniel kept the horses at a slow walk, they broke up this morning's bales and scattered the hay in a zigzag pattern that over the winter would seed the entire field for the spring.

Over his shoulder, Daniel said to Cale, "You're keeping late hours. Where were you that you didn't get in until nearly midnight? Lovina was worried."

Cale grinned and snipped the binder twine with a pair of

pliers. "She didn't need to worry. I was in the holiest of holies —the bishop's kitchen."

Zach nearly took a header off the back of the wagon when the horse stepped forward.

"What were you doing there?" Adam asked. "Baptism classes?"

"Ha ha, very funny. I was baptized when I was twenty. No, I walked Ruby home over that shortcut, which turned out to be a bad idea. She slipped and fell, so I carried her home."

All three of his cousins stopped their work to stare. Zach was the first to regain his equilibrium. "Is she all right?"

"I think so. I guess she strained the same ligament once playing baseball. Lucky I was there. If she'd gone down like that alone in the middle of the night, I don't know if she'd have made it home."

Here Zach had been searching the house to find her so he could walk her home, and all the while she'd been with Cale.

And gotten hurt. Hurt enough to be carried home. "Is she going to see a doctor?"

"Not a lot they can do with a ligament," Daniel said, clucking to the horse so it would move forward once more.

"Her mother put liniment on it and wrapped it," Cale told them. "Ruby used a cane to get upstairs, so it might not be that serious."

"You didn't carry her upstairs, too?" came out of Zach's mouth before his brain could stop it.

Cale chuckled as if Zach had been ribbing him. "When I'm with a girl and she gets carried away, it won't be in front of her father."

Zach was still reeling from the image of Ruby in Cale's arms, being carried home in the moonlight. If ever there was a romantic gesture to get a woman's attention, that would be it.

Unlike Zach's lack of any kind of gesture, as he bumbled around outside on the deck and wondered what was keeping her.

Cale Kuepfer, it turned out, had been keeping her.

He couldn't bring himself to speak to the man anymore, so he concentrated instead on tossing feed as if his own survival depended on it, not just that of the cows. With the extra pair of hands, the feed was soon distributed. He and Daniel brought up the rear as the others rode toward the barn. He turned up his collar with one hand as the wind tried to find its way down his neck.

Dat had been right. The temperature was dropping again and the clouds moving in. At least the bench wagon would get to Keims' before the weather got too bad.

Daniel saw the wagon backed into the barn, then waved, heading home for breakfast. Just to be on the safe side, Zach backed the horse under the hay hole, then climbed up to toss down tomorrow's bales. Adam gave him a hand to heave them onto the wagon bed. Both of them knew that if it was snowing in the morning, the less time it took to get the feed out to the cattle, the better.

"What's going on with you?" his brother asked quietly. When Zach didn't answer, he went on, "*Ischt okay.* We're on our own. Daniel took Cale down to the house."

"Nothing's going on."

"Getting snippy with our cousin isn't nothing. Something's eating you."

Zach kneed a bale into place in the wagon bed and bent to pick up another one.

"Did Cale do something? Something to do with Ruby?" Adam asked.

The bale settled into place with a *whump*. "What kind of

fool lets a woman fall on the trail and hurt herself so bad she has to be carried home?"

"The kind of fool following a woman who knew the way, I expect," Adam said mildly. "Not a lot he could do in the dark, and she knows the trail blindfolded. It was just a misstep."

"Still. Nothing like topping it off with a grand romantic gesture."

Adam was silent. "You think there's something going on there?"

"*Ja.*"

"With *Ruby?*"

A spurt of irritation curled Zach's hands into the bale of hay. "Don't sound so surprised. Ruby is a beautiful girl. More than that, she has a beautiful soul."

"And she's the bishop's daughter." Adam nodded thoughtfully. "A man could do worse than court a girl like that."

"He's not courting her."

Adam's brows rose at his tone. "If he's not, he's giving a good impression of it. And what about this is getting under your skin? I know you and Ruby are *gut* friends. Are you mad that she's spending time with someone else?"

"She can do what she wants. I've got no hold on her."

But Adam had that face now—the face he got when at last he understood a mechanical problem or what was ailing a sick animal. Or, Zach suddenly realized, when his brother was applying his own recent experience with love to Zach's pathetic lack of it.

"Zachariah. You *are* jealous. Because you want more than to be *gut* friends. You want to court Ruby yourself."

"What's wrong with that?" he mumbled, shoving at the bale of hay.

"Nothing in the world." Adam paused to heave one on top of it. "How long have you felt this way?"

All my life. "It just became ... real ... this past week or so."

"When Cale came on the scene. Does she know how you feel?" When Zach shook his head, Adam leaned on the side of the wagon as if it were all that was holding him up under the weight of this revelation. "This whole week is looking different to me now. I thought Cale was like that with everyone. But he wasn't. He treats Ruby differently than anyone else."

"Like *what* with everyone?"

"Kind, helpful, lending a hand with a smile. Our sisters think he's the best thing since sliced bread."

"You're not helping, *Bruder*."

Adam laughed and gripped his shoulder briefly. "I'm a fine one to talk. It took a miracle for me to stop being blind and realize I'd been in love with Kate in my heart and soul, while my body thought it was in love with Elizabeth. But when that moment came, it changed how I saw everything."

"It has for me, too," Zach admitted. "But I didn't know I cared so much until it was too late. Now what do I do? Mamm says I need to talk to her. But how can I when Cale is carrying her home like some knight in shining armor, and I didn't even know she was hurt?"

"Well, you know two things now. One, that you care. And two, that Cale is going home in two weeks."

"What if he decides to stay?" he asked miserably. "He could hire on as a cabinetmaker with the Petersheim outfit."

"And leave his father in the lurch? That wouldn't say anything good about him. But you're right, it is a risk. So what you need to do is tell Ruby the truth. And when Cale sees that she only has eyes for you, he'll climb in the taxi-van and take his broken heart back to Prince Edward Island."

Adam clapped him on the back and went out, leaving Zach to unhitch the horses from the loaded wagon with a heart just as burdened.

Tell Ruby the truth.

But what if he was already too late? What if Cale had succeeded in capturing that sweet, loyal, loving heart with his helpful habits and grand gestures? In that case, telling her the truth would only make her feel sorry for him, and he didn't think he could bear that.

On the other hand, a man ought to be *deemiedich*. He would be all kinds of a fool if he let fear of a little humility keep him from speaking the truth in his heart. He'd been all kinds of a fool already. It was time to stop, and become the man who was worthy of her.

But what could he do? One of the things he'd always appreciated about being Amish was that people put more stock in a person's actions than their words. Words could be misunderstood, discounted, disbelieved, but actions could be counted on. What action of his would tell Ruby how he felt?

He spent the rest of the day cleaning the barn and wracking his brain. Seth and Gideon came out to help him with the barn, though they weren't much help with the Ruby part since he couldn't talk about it. But they were *gut* company, particularly since he didn't have to tell them what to do—they were experienced hands on the 4 Winds Ranch in New Mexico.

And he learned that Gideon was smitten with Ruby, too, and planned to give Cale a little competition.

Zach smiled to himself. While they were competing with each other, he'd find a way to get close enough to touch Ruby's heart. So he pretended to encourage Gideon just enough to keep his cousin interested and talking about it.

Over the next two days, he kept an eye on Cale and Gideon both. When one looked like he might stroll down the lane to see how the bishop's daughter was doing, the other found that he needed help with some task—or rather, each found that Dat needed their help.

For Zach, Ruby's absence on the Circle M was like a missing limb. If he'd ever taken her cheerful presence for granted before, he certainly wasn't now. He missed her every minute. How many times in two days he'd come in for *Kaffee* or supper with some little bit of news to share with her, and remembered with a thump of disappointment that she wasn't there? He'd seen a trio of swans flying farther south—his first thought had been to tell her about it. His second thought had been to draw their beautiful shapes as they stretched their necks out toward Idaho, so he could show her.

Why don't you draw something?

It was almost as though someone had spoken inside his head. The agitation that had kept him doing ranch work right up until he had to leave for the big Christmas Eve dinner at Daniel and Lovina's settled into conviction, even as he talked with his relatives and laughed with his cousins.

Of course he would draw something. Why had it taken two days to figure that out? Ruby was always asking if he'd drawn anything lately, and he'd pull out his sketchbook and show her —three sparrows clinging to a sunflower seed head while they hunted down the last seed—Malena and Alden folding a long tablecloth together with it stretched out between them—a view over his mother's shoulder as she looked down at little Deborah sleeping on her chest.

Christmas Day was tomorrow. He had never given Ruby a gift before, but this year he would, even if he sat up half the night to finish it.

And he knew just what the subject would be.

Christmas Day

FALLING SNOW WHISPERED AGAINST THE WINDOW WHEN Ruby woke Christmas morning. You'd have thought that with all the ice Mamm had insisted she keep on her ankle that she would have been tired of cold things, but there was something about a Christmas snowfall that was magical. And these were not the dry soaplike flakes that usually fell in the high country, but were actual snowflakes with patterns in them. They lasted a moment on the glass, then melted, only to be replaced by a dozen more.

They didn't have a tree, of course, but Mamm and Aendi Rosemary had gathered fir boughs yesterday to lay along the mantel, and Ruby had bought fat red candles with bases as big as her palm at the candle shop in town to set among the greenery. In the center, Mamm had a hexagonal lantern whose one side opened like a door, and a white candle went in there.

Dat had already lit the stove, so the living room was warm for when her brothers and their families woke and the children ran downstairs in their nightclothes. She lit the candles on the mantel, and the lamps on the end tables, but not the big Coleman hanging from the ceiling in the kitchen. They didn't make a big ceremony of gifts, but they had wrapped a few special things for the *Kinner*, now sitting on the coffee table waiting for them.

A soft knock came at the kitchen door. Mamm and Dat were upstairs, so Ruby went to answer it. Through the glass, all she could distinguish was that it was a man, until he turned into the light and she saw it was Zach.

Joy flared up inside her like a match had been struck, to be followed immediately afterward by something that almost felt like grief. She swallowed and opened the door.

"Guder mariye." She stepped aside, inviting him in, but he shook his head.

"I have to get back to feed the cows, but I wanted to give you this." He laid a scroll of paper in her palm, tied with a length of narrow ribbon that had clearly come from the spool she'd used to tie up the cake favors at Rebecca's wedding. *"Frehlicher Grischdaag,* Ruby."

He turned to go, but she stopped him. "Wait. I have something for you, too."

She hurried over to the small wooden box that held her crafting things, and took an envelope from it. *"Frehlicher Grischdaag,* Zach. Open it when you get home."

He gave her one of his real smiles, the kind that warmed you up from the inside. And then he was gone, his boots crunching in the snow until he disappeared into the dark and she realized she was still standing there in the open doorway in her stocking feet.

Hastily, she closed the door, limped over to pour herself a cup of *Kaffee,* and took his gift into the living room. She sat in her corner of the sofa and slid the ribbon off, then unrolled the paper—heavier than normal letter paper, stiffer than newsprint. Paper from his sketchbook.

She drew a long breath, smoothing it flat.

There they were, the two of them, skating. Their backs were to the viewer, because Zach believed that sketching a person's face was creating a graven image that could be made an idol of. But his hands held both of hers in the classic

THE AMISH COWBOY'S HOME

skater's hold they had never actually done in real life. His face was tilted down as he listened to something she was telling him, her face tilted up. In one more breath, the two pencilled figures might kiss.

In fact, the entire picture breathed longing. His body, inclined toward hers. Her own, leaning upward the way she'd seen Mamm kiss Dat in passing once, when they thought she was in another room. Their feet keeping time together on the ice, the right foot's weight on the blade, the left in the air, about to swing forward.

And such detail! Every pleat in her *Kapp*, the fringe on the ends of her scarf, the dimple in his left cheek as he smiled—just a hook of the pencil had captured it forever, that ephemeral dimple she loved. His clever pencil had captured them exactly as they were—and as they had never been.

For this picture showed two people in love. Two people for whom there was no one else in the world, for whom no one else existed off that enchanted page.

Her gaze moved to the bottom, where he had written in his spiky hand, *Best friends make the best partners. Merry Christmas.*

Once, when she was little, one of her brothers had been pushing her on the swing that used to hang from a big pine in the back yard. He'd turned his back just for a moment, and she'd fallen off and landed hard on the ground. It had knocked the breath out of her. And she'd been so embarassed and ashamed at her own clumsiness that she'd burst into tears, lying there trying to breathe, tears leaking out of the corners of her eyes.

She felt a little like that now.

Best friends.

In this picture she had seen *special* friends—no, more than that, she'd seen two people completely in love. Every line in the two sketched bodies declared it, only to be bluntly contradicted by the message at the bottom. So obviously they weren't declaring any such thing. She was simply reading far more into this little drawing than he meant or that actually existed anywhere except in her starved heart.

Best friends.

Yes, they had been that. It was nice of him to say so.

But now? How could they be best friends now?

Sitting in the quiet living room in the flickering candlelight, the snow whispering at the windows, Ruby looked into the future and did not think she could face what she saw. Because someday, *Gott* would bring someone into Zach's life and they would fall in love. He would take her home to the Circle M and Ruby would have to see them every other Sunday in church. There she would be, moving down the bench as, year after year, the single *Maedscher* got younger and she got older. She would stay in this house, looking after her parents as they aged while Zach and his wife brought first one, then two, then three or four children into the world. Proof of their love and of the rightness of *der Herr*'s choice for them.

Her heart seemed to squeeze with pain.

The fact was, she didn't have the strength to live that life. She couldn't watch Zach Miller love someone else when she had never loved anyone but him.

But that had to change. The reason was right here in her hand.

Best friends.

He would never see her as a woman he could love. The woman he could marry. Have children with. He would always see her as his friend, the bishop's daughter.

She simply couldn't bear it.

How was she going to get through this day, carrying so

much pain? How could she get through the next day, seeing him at church, and the next week, and on into the new year?

The drawing rolled itself up in her hands as she closed her eyes.

Dear Father, how am I going to live like this? Hilfe mich. Let me know Thy will for my life. If it's not being Zach's wife, then I humbly beg Thee to show me Thy plan for me. Help me endure this pain and come out on the other side with willingness. I pray these things in Thy Son's holy name.

She heard her parents now, talking quietly upstairs, wondering if the children were up yet. She didn't have the heart to open the door of the stove and throw the little drawing in, so she rolled it up more tightly and hid it on the mantel, behind the lantern with the white candle in it. Amid the fronds of cedar and pine, it looked like an unlit candle.

By the time her parents came downstairs, she was out in the kitchen, putting a pan of milk on the stove to make hot chocolate for the *Kinner*.

If she had to learn to be the spinster *Aendi* in the family, she may as well begin now.

11

CHRISTMAS DAY

FOR ZACH, Christmas on the Circle M was the happiest time of year, celebrating the birth of Jesus and celebrating the *Bopplin* in the family as well. Now that his brothers and sisters were pairing up and would be creating families of their own, it seemed to him that not only was the big living room overlooking the river filled with chatter and laughter, it was filled with hope and a sense of a joyous future, too.

From upstairs, he couldn't distinguish individual voices, but he could hear the cheery racket, made even fuller by the addition of his extended family. They weren't really in the habit of giving many gifts anymore—the babies were too young, but Joel's were waiting for him when Daniel and Lovina brought him up to the big house.

And Zach? He had Ruby's gift to him. Not for the first time this morning, he smoothed it between his fingers. He wasn't quite sure what to make of it, but then, when she'd made it, obviously she hadn't yet seen the drawing. She'd given him a bookmark that one friend might give another—she had crocheted a ribbon of lace out of a fine white thread that looked like a row of snowflakes, and mounted it on a strip of green paper just the length of a book's page. Down the side of the paper were written in black ink the words, FOR ALL I TRUST HIM, creating the acronym for the word FAITH. It wasn't what he would call a personal gift—she could have given one just like it to his mother—but if she had meant to encourage him spiritually, she'd certainly succeeded. And the fact that it was handmade, the layers pressed between two sheets of laminate with a hot iron to protect her work, meant that she intended him to use it.

And to think of her each time he did.

She would have seen his drawing of the two of them by now. What would her response be?

He could hardly wait until after lunch, when the *Gmee* would spend the afternoon making Christmas Day visits to those nearest them. With the fresh fall of snow, the Millers might only see the bishop's family, who were close enough that they could walk. They might not even see Joshua and Sarah and Nathan, if the county blade didn't make it out here today.

He walked down the stairs and settled himself at the back of the group as Dat opened the big Bible, written in *hoch Deitsch*, that had come with Daadi Miller fifty years ago when the Siksika district had first been settled by the Amish. The room quieted. Even baby Deborah on Mamm's shoulder sucked her little fist, gazing at Dat.

"Now when Jesus was born in Bethlehem of Judaea in the days of Herod the king, behold, there came wise men from the east to Jerusalem..."

They would hear the story of Jesus' birth again in church tomorrow, but there was something about the quality of Dat's voice, a kind of awe, that drew them in. His own emotion as he read aloud made their family part of the story, as though they were the shepherds watching by night, and seeing the star in the east. The truth was, every one who confessed His name was a part of the story, on and on through the centuries of belief.

If anything could comfort and encourage Zach amid the messiness of his personal life, it was that.

When Dat closed the Bible, he bowed his head. A rustle swept through the room as everyone followed suit.

"Father in Heaven, we bow before you today to thank You for the gift of Your Son, who lived to please You, and who shed his blood to save and ransom us. As we celebrate His birth together today, let us keep our eyes and our thoughts on Him, not on any worldly gift we might receive that is just a shadow and an echo of Thy greatest gift. Be with us as we fellowship together today, and find joy in our service to Thee. We ask these things in Thy Son's holy name."

"Amen," Zach murmured.

When Dat lifted his head and smiled at Joel, it was the signal for Malena, Emily, Jenny, and Susanna to leave their seats and head out to the kitchen to put the finishing touches on breakfast. Joel dug into his little pile of presents, the one from Mamm and Dat wrapped in butcher paper on which Zach had drawn a family of Canada geese having their own Christmas dinner in a field that looked strangely like the Circle M's home pasture, with Hester the buggy horse nodding over the fence in approval.

Joel loved the drawing as much as the hand-knit boot socks, muffler, and mittens his grandmother had made, and the copy of *Birds of North America* his parents gave him.

Kate Weaver had received a gift, too. It had come in the mail two days ago from her sister in Whinburg Township. Delight suffused her face as she lifted out a set of kitchen towels, clearly meant for her hope chest, each one trimmed with a narrow border of pieced fabric diamonds for a little bit of decoration. Zach didn't know what the pattern was called, but it brought such a happy smile to Kate's face that it clearly represented more than something to dry dishes with.

Something that had gone very wrong between the two sisters seemed to have been put right at last. Maybe Elizabeth was so happy with Andrew King that she no longer resented her sister's happiness with Adam. Zach could only hope so.

Kate and Adam cuddled on the sofa, with Rebecca and Noah beside them.

"The newlyweds and the nearlyweds," Seth Miller leaned in to whisper to Zach.

"It's the best Christmas gift of all to know that three of my *Kinner* are so happy in God's choice of their spouse," Mamm said, her eyes glistening. "I wish Joshua and Sara could be here."

"They'll come as soon as the plow goes through." Dat smiled at her, then turned his attention to Noah and Rebecca. "I hope you won't feel in any hurry to move out. Once your wedding visits are done in the valley and away, then there's plenty of time to think it over."

"*Denki*, Dat," Rebecca said.

"I was talking with *mei Bruder* Simeon at the wedding," Noah told them. "He has a feeling that Andrew's not coming out to see us married means he plans to stay in Whinburg Township. Sim is certain that our carpentry business is going to be down by one."

"A chance, maybe, for someone in the valley to sign on with you," Tobias suggested.

"That's a possibility," Noah agreed. "Too bad you and

Gideon and Seth would rather wrangle cows than swing a hammer."

"A man can do both," Dat pointed out, taking Deborah from Mamm. "Look at you, chasing and roping calves at roundup as if you'd been cowboying all your life."

Noah grinned and conceded the point, but Zach noticed he didn't commit himself. He also noticed Adam's relief. Noah's helping his new family wrangle cattle was one thing, but carpentry was what he was trained for and was skilled at. And goodness knew they could use builders with skills in the valley—especially with newlyweds needing to establish homes of their own.

"Don't tempt my boys away from cowboying, Noah King." Rachel laughed as she rose from her chair. "Not until we see whether the *gut Gott* has changed His mind about where He wants our branch of the family to be." Her gaze strayed to the river valley where she'd grown up, and the snowy mountains beyond, then returned to the crowded living room. "I don't think even this house expected to have three whole families jammed in all at one time. But I think it's a joy and a privilege to be here with you all while I wait on *Gott* to show us the path He wants for us."

That seemed to be the signal for a tide of family to wash into the kitchen and see how breakfast was coming along.

Zach was able to face Cale over his huge plate of food— which the *Youngie* ate off their laps to leave the big kitchen table for the older and younger—with something approaching cordiality. And it was even sincere. He couldn't blame the guy for trying to get Ruby's attention, without the years of friendship with her to give him an advantage. The kind of trust that Zach and Ruby had built up with each other over a lifetime couldn't be Cale's, either, no matter how confident and self-

assured he was. Ruby might appreciate that in a man, but what she valued was someone who understood her, who wouldn't expect her to be a visible leader—she found ways to get things done in the background. She was like the glue that held groups of people together and got them organized, whether it was Sisters' Day or a quilting frolic or simply cleaning an entire house for church.

Would Cale understand that, despite her abilities, she needed quiet time? Zach hadn't seen any evidence that he might. Only a man who knew Ruby as well as Zach did could make her happy.

He had made the first move. The next would be up to her. Maybe even this afternoon.

IF SHE HADN'T HAD THIS STRAINED TENDON, WOULD SHE BE over at the Circle M today, visiting? Ruby was in the habit of honesty with herself, and she had to admit that after receiving the drawing from Zach, she might not have had the courage to walk into his home.

What woman would go on purpose to be reminded that all her hopes and dreams had never been based on reality, that the man she cared for would never care for her in return? Even she knew when to stop running into the side of the barn when it was not going to move no matter what she did.

So here she was in the big living room in Dat's armchair, her foot up on an ottoman with an ice pack on it, Daadi's cane handy for when she needed to get up. Mamm hadn't even let her try to do the dishes, but had practically set her down like a pillow herself, and told her to enjoy their visitors when they came.

"The county blade finally got out here," Aendi Rosemary reported, bringing Ruby a mug of tea and honey. "And with the clouds lifting, I expect a fair number might stop by."

Christmas visits were a tradition that Ruby usually enjoyed. Despite her reputation for being quiet and not very talkative, she did like people. Some people were easier to talk to at length than others, that was all.

Lunch had barely been cleared off the table by her sisters-in-law and plates of cookies and cake and pies arranged in their place, when a knock came at the door and in came a host of Millers. They came, and they came, and Ruby couldn't help but wonder how on earth Zach was managing with a constant crowd this size in the house.

But that was pointless, wasn't it? Wondering about him, being concerned for him—she needed to put away childish things and look into her own future as an adult.

She'd barely got this admonition settled inside herself when Zach materialized out of the crowd removing coats and boots, and claimed the chair next to hers. "*Frehlicher Grischdaag* again, Ruby—*wie geht's?*"

She opened her mouth to say something, but Cale practically bounded across the room to secure the wooden chair on her other side, and then goodness sakes if Gideon Miller didn't pick up a ladder-back chair with one hand, swing it around, and plunk himself down on it backward, grinning at her over his crossed arms.

"How is the ankle?" Cale asked, eyeing the ice pack. "Getting better?" Before she could reply, he said, "I've been kicking myself ever since Tuesday that I let it happen. I could have grabbed you and prevented your fall."

"You were five or six feet behind me," she reminded him. "There was nothing you could have done—it was my own

fault. You'd think I'd know by now that mud means the ground isn't frozen anymore." She paused, then with a spurt of courage, said, "Thank you for bringing me that book. I finished it. It's on the counter by the kitchen door, if you'd return it for me."

Beaming, Cale asked, "Did you like it?"

Zach looked as though someone had spun him around the way they used to as kids in Blind Man's Bluff, and he'd lost his sense of direction. "You brought her a book?"

"*Ja*, one of the Lucy Maud Montgomery books. I saw them on the shelf and Naomi thought Ruby would like to read one."

"Which one?" Zach said.

"*Anne of the Island*," Ruby said. "I've read *Anne of Green Gables*, of course, but I didn't realize there were so many more."

"You missed the one in between," Emily told her brother, sitting beside him. "*Anne of Avonlea*. Why didn't you bring it? You went straight from Anne at twelve to Anne at eighteen or something, when all the fun disasters like the baking powder story and the escaped cow are in the second book."

"Because the third one has lots of stuff about PEI, and—" He twinkled at Ruby. "—it's the one where Anne and Gilbert finally get engaged."

Out of the corner of her eye, Ruby saw the color leave Zach's tanned face. What was the matter with him? Was he sick?

What had Cale just—*oh*.

Oh my.

Hot color scalded Ruby's cheeks and if she could have leaped up and run, she would have.

Gideon was looking pained. "Why didn't you give her

something sensible, like Zane Grey? Or Louis L'Amour? Something we all know. Cattle. Horses."

"She said she liked this one, cowboy. Besides, it's something *we* know." He indicated Emily with a tilt of his head. "Our own province."

"Can I get you a plate, Ruby?" Emily asked.

"Oh—*denki*, I—"

Before she could finish, three young men leaped to their feet and galloped out to the kitchen. Emily laughed, tipping her head back the way Malena did in pure enjoyment. Then with a glance at Little Joe, she seemed to recollect herself, and lowered her head. "Was it something I said?" she finally got out, her dark eyes still laughing even if her face was straight.

"You said *plate*. Maybe they heard *date*, and it frightened them away."

That set Emily off again, until Dat really did look over in case he might get in on the joke, and she sobered up with a gasp.

"It's all right, Emily," Ruby said. "My father loves a good laugh."

"Oh—I—are you sure?" It didn't seem nearly as funny to Emily now. "Our bishop says that laughing out loud like that draws attention, and it's not becoming in a woman."

"Then your bishop ought to read Genesis, where Sarah laughed. They might have called her on it, but she said, 'God hath made me to laugh, so that all that hear will laugh with me.'"

Emily grinned. "I'll bring that up the next time he gives me that disapproving face from across the yard."

Zach, Cale, and Gideon all returned in a herd, to thrust three plates of goodies under Ruby's nose. Calmly, Emily took one of the plates. "*Denki*, Cale. How nice of you to think of your *Schweschder*, who did *not* have two helpings of stew at lunch."

Zach clearly expected Ruby to accept his plate, which held only two things—mincemeat pie with a scoop of ice cream, and a butter tart. She adored mincemeat pie, and only got it at this time of year. But there he was, with that confident look on his face. The look that said, *I know what you like better than anyone because we've been friends for so long.*

Friendship was a pale substitute for what her heart longed for.

She accepted Gideon's plate, which at least had shortbread bars and the scrumptious date-with-oatmeal-topping concoction that Mamm called *matrimonial cake*. On second thought, maybe that hadn't been the wisest decision. Gideon lit up as though she'd given him a present, and she wondered if he was maybe sending her a message, too.

Too late now.

But since the cake was delicious, she ate the whole piece.

12

IT TOOK Zach a full ten seconds to realize Ruby was not going to eat the pie he'd brought for her. The ice cream was already melting, so there was only one thing left to do.

Pretend he'd brought it for himself. With every bite, questions crowded his tongue that he couldn't ask in front of these two donkeys to whom he happened to be related. But Ruby seemed to have no shortage of questions.

"Is the Island still the way it was in the book?" she asked Cale with a smile. "Fields stretching down to the sea, and beautiful sunsets, and the wind off the Gulf blowing through the pines?"

"That part is," he said, around a piece of shortbread. "If there were only Amish and Old Order Mennonites living there today, with our horses and buggies, even Montgomery might still recognize it."

"But add in modern highways and speeding cars and tourists," Emily said, "and it's a different place. Many of our folk were able to buy land at a pretty good price, compared to

Ontario. The growing season is longer than it is out here in the West, so many do still farm."

"But if you're not a farmer, you do something different," Cale went on. "Cabinetmaking is only one thing. There is a shop that does mechanical conversions in the district near Montague. We could really use someone to do that in Lorgan Township—it's a long drive. And a couple of our young men work on the lobster and mussel farms." He quirked an eyebrow at Emily.

"I want to open a quilt shop with a couple of the *Maedscher*," she said in a lower tone, as though it might have been a secret. "But we haven't found just the right place yet. It needs to be close to a main road, maybe even in the village."

"You don't want to sell them out of your house?" Gideon asked. "They do that a lot in Pennsylvania."

"We could," Emily said, "but all our parents can see is strangers tramping all around the place taking pictures, like they do in Pennsylvania."

"Dat's family is all from Strasburg, though he was born in Ontario," Cale put in. "He and the bishop are trying to balance the good that the tourists bring to the community with how intrusive it can be for the *Gmee*. Folks from Pennsylvania might be used to it, but folks from Aylmer sure aren't."

"But neither of you plans to leave and go somewhere else to make a living—or a home?" Ruby asked.

"Neh," Emily said with a smile. "I love the Island. Sure, the winters are cold and the spring is wet. But the summer and autumn are so beautiful they make up for everything."

"Then again, it's not you out there on the lobster boat, pulling up traps for the restaurants in a howling gale," Cale pointed out.

"Or you either, safe in your nice warm shop," she retorted.

"But the Steiner boys—all five of them—love being out on the water no matter how awful it is. In the summer, they're part fish, always going swimming."

"Are the roads really red?" Ruby asked with a smile. "Like in *Anne of Green Gables*?"

"*Ja*, they are," Cale told her. "So are the cliffs, and the beaches in many places."

"In some places near us, the beaches are so shallow and go out so far that the moon snails lay their eggs there," Emily said. "You've never seen anything so enchanting as little baby moon snails creeping over the red sandstone underwater, feeling out the big world and wondering what giant creature it is whose feet are blocking their way."

Ruby laughed, and with the animation and interest in her face, something chilly settled in Zach's stomach.

"But what makes them red?" she persisted. "Anne never did find out when she asked Matthew."

"Iron oxide," Cale told her. "The soil is *gut*, and I think our people came at the right time a few years ago. The *Englisch* folks who wanted a different life in Charlottetown made it possible for Mamm and Dat to have the life they wanted. Dat's brother and his four sons farm their acres, and they lease ours."

"So you're not going to be a farmer?" Gideon asked.

"*Neh*, not me." Cale flexed his hands, then picked up the pumpkin streusel cake that was all that remained on his plate. "*Gott* gave Dat and me a talent, so we honor Him by exercising it. And He allows us to prosper."

"Aaron and Jacob have always been part dirt, part boy," Emily said with a laugh. "They might go to work for our *Onkel* next year. They haven't been working out so well in the shop."

Cale pretended to shudder. "Mamm laid down the law after the sawblade incident."

"I don't want to know." Ruby put her hands over her ears to make her point. "What do you do in the winter? You don't stop work, obviously."

"Do you mean for fun?" Cale asked.

"Ja." A smile lingered on her lips.

The cold feeling in Zach's stomach chilled a little more. Something was coming, he could feel it. And there was no way he could stop it outside of making some kind of scene.

"All kinds of things, like you do here," Emily said. "Ice skating, and hockey."

"Cross-country skiing? Snow-shoeing?" Zach managed.

"Those aren't fun," Ruby contradicted him, as if he should know better. "Those are simply a way to get around when the horses can't manage the roads."

Emily's hand went to her mouth, then fluttered to her lap, as if she realized she could speak freely here. "Our bishop would have kittens if he saw us cross-country skiing," she said, her voice just above a whisper. "And nobody has snowshoes, so it hasn't occurred to him to put those in the *Ordnung* yet."

"How does a person get to work then?" Gideon wanted to know. "I mean, if a man didn't have a shop on his place?"

"It's never quite as bad as that," Cale said, "and the townships are pretty good about plowing. They even plow the gravel roads."

"Your bishop sounds very..." Ruby glanced at her father, whose booming laugh had just rung out over something Aendi Rachel had said. "Strict."

"He is, but we still find ways to have fun." Cale grinned at his sister. "Even when we're courting."

But if he'd intended to crack a joke, it fell flat. Emily's

smile faded away along with all the color in her face, and her gaze dropped to their empty plates. "Would anyone like a refill?" She jumped up and held out a hand.

Zach shook his head and let her take his plate away into the kitchen.

To save the moment, in her considerate way, Ruby said, "It sounds *wunderbaar* on Prince Edward Island. Wouldn't it be an adventure to visit someday? It seems as far away as a story-book, but from what you say, I know it really isn't."

"A week's travel, but it's worth it when you get there."

Here it came. Zach's gaze bounced frantically around the bishop's big living room, looking for help and finding none.

Cale said, "Why don't you come for a visit, Ruby? There's lots of room. When we built the house, my older brother and sister were still at home. We use their rooms for guests now."

"How kind of you to invite me on your own without your parents' knowledge," she teased. "But it's an awfully long way to go, *nix*? Thousands of miles."

Zach thought he might be able to breathe. "I looked it up when we heard the family might be coming," he croaked. He cleared his throat. "It's three thousand miles."

Gideon whistled. "A long way to go for a visit. You'd have to stay for a year to make it worthwhile."

Cale rose. "I'm for a cup of coffee. Can I get you one, Ruby?"

"*Ja, denki.*"

Please let this little travelogue be over. But Zach didn't dare leave, even when Joel dragged Gideon and Emily with him to see something outside the window. Probably some kind of bird, which he was obsessed with lately.

Zach seized his chance before any of the married folks came over to ask after Ruby's ankle. "*Denki* for your gift this morning," he said in a tone that carried only to her ears. "I put it in one of my books right away. I hope you liked yours, too."

"*Ja*, I did. You draw so well, Zach."

Her tone didn't quite ring true, as though he'd given her a picture of a horse. Or a flower. Or an egg. He had no choice but to press her. "And what did you think of the message?"

"It's nice to know we're best friends."

That was *not* the point.

"I like that part, too. But what about the rest?"

She tilted her head to look up at him. "Skating partners? It's nice—lifelike."

Nice?

"I meant more than skating partners." He meant *partners* in the fullest sense of the word. "I meant—"

Cale reappeared like a barn cat at milking time, a cup of coffee in each hand. "Sorry I didn't get you one, Zach," he said in apology as he handed one to Ruby.

Could he have made a broader hint that Zach was an unwelcome third?

Zach glanced to where Emily had been at the window, but she was talking to her parents and the bishop now. No help was coming from that quarter. This was torture. If only he could spirit Ruby away somewhere and talk to her in private! But neither was he moving from this chair as long as Ruby sat in the armchair next to it, no matter who else came to interrupt.

She leaned over and removed the ice pack on her ankle. "Can you put this back outside, Zach?"

So much for not moving. But he'd do anything she asked. "Save my place," he said with a smile, and took the ice pack outside. On the porch Sadie had an icebox straight out of the forties, with three cubelike metal cupboards one of top of the other. The family no longer cut ice for summer, but in the winter it acted as a freezer, when the external temperatures rarely climbed above thirty degrees.

When he returned, any hopes of resuming his chair by her side faded at the sight of Emily sitting down and leaning toward Ruby as though she had news. He'd only been gone half a minute.

But something big had happened in those thirty seconds. Ruby seemed to be frozen in place, her coffee mug halfway to her lips. She looked as though a hay bale had fallen on her head and stunned her.

Cale wore the most infuriating grin, as though he figured he'd just given her the present she'd been wishing for all her life. "We leave the day after Old Christmas," he was saying, which Zach couldn't understand, because they all knew that.

"It's true, Ruby," Emily said eagerly. "I just talked to my parents and the bishop. You can ask them if you like. If you feel able to travel home with us next week, my parents have invited you to stay."

"For as long as you want." Cale met Zach's disbelieving gaze over Ruby's head, his eyes glittering with humor and triumph.

There was a roaring sound in Zach's ears. He could barely hear Ruby's soft voice as she said, "I can't just say *ja* or *neh* this minute. Maybe we should talk about it some other time, when there isn't a houseful of people."

"Better yet, tomorrow after the singing, when we have a five-mile drive together," Cale teased her. "Think that will be enough time for me to convince you to come?"

Now Zach knew what that roaring sound was, loud as one of the cataracts that formed on the sides of the mountains during runoff in the spring. It was the sound of his hopes, his dreams, his very future, all crashing down around his ears.

𝕬

IT TOOK ALL OF RUBY'S SELF-CONTROL TO KEEP A SMILE ON her face as Zach bolted through the groups of people and out into the kitchen. A moment later came the sound of the back door closing. If she could have, she'd have followed him and, like a dozen other times, found some quiet, sunny corner of the porch where together, they could breathe and recover from the onslaught of people.

Because it felt like an onslaught—not just the crowd, but this teasing, laughing upending of all her plans for the winter. This happy assumption that she would love to hop in the taxi-van and travel three thousand miles from home on a whim, for the sake of an adventure. The least they could have done was ask her what she thought first, before blurting it all out in front of her father, for goodness sake!

"What's the matter, Ruby?" Emily's eyes searched her face, her smile fading. "Don't you think it's a great plan?"

"She's having second thoughts," Cale said. "We'd better nip that in the bud, *nix*?"

"I haven't even had a chance for *first* thoughts," Ruby said. In a gentler tone, she went on, "You didn't even ask me if I wanted to go."

"Don't you?" Now Emily was looking downright worried. "Did I overstep? I wanted to make sure it would be all right with Mamm and Dat before I extended the invitation, that's all. You have to forgive *mei Bruder*—when he runs away with an idea, he's like a horse with the bit in his teeth."

"It's just ... so sudden," she said. In a minute she would cry from sheer frustration and overwhelmed emotions. "It's ever so kind of you—please thank your parents for the invitation—I have to think—"

She grasped the cane and struggled out of the chair, desperate to escape. Was Zach still outside? No, she couldn't go chasing after him in front of everybody. In front of Cale, who was to take her home tomorrow night. Who honestly couldn't be blamed for thinking that, after all her eager questions, she really was interested in seeing the island they loved so much, and hadn't just been doing it to make Zach jealous.

Oh, *ja*, and hadn't she just succeeded. So well that he was probably halfway home by now.

"I—I need to rest," she said a little incoherently, and hobbled through the crowd to the stairs. With the help of both the cane and the bannister, she was able to climb them without falling on her face, and in another moment, she was safe in her room with the door closed.

She fell onto the bed. What sweet relief to be alone!

She arranged the second pillow under her ankle, and lay back to gaze at the familiar planks of the ceiling while a beam of pale winter sunshine came and went across her body with the waving of the pine branches outside. Her room was the last on the right, looking out into the woods, and well out of the way of normal family traffic. Especially today, with *Kinner* and in-laws filling the other bedrooms with happy chatter and the occasional pounding of running feet. It got cold in here in the winter when she was the only child home and the heat coming up the stairs didn't quite reach to the end of the hall, but at times like this, when the rest of the family were home, she was willing to pull up an extra quilt if it meant having this little bit of privacy.

Just her and the snowy pines.

And her thoughts, tumbling over each other like the clothes in a dryer at the *Englisch* laundromat in town.

She let them tumble. Eventually they would run out of energy and arrange themselves in some sensible order. Maybe then she might be able to come to a decision. But right now—

A soft tap came at the door. *Ach, neh!* Her whole being seemed to sink into the mattress. Was it too much to ask for just five minutes to herself?

The tap came again. She couldn't pretend to be asleep, because then they'd only open the door to check. And she couldn't tell them to go away, because that was rude and unbecoming to the bishop's daughter in the bishop's house.

With a sigh, she said, "*Ja, kumm* in."

Mamm slipped through the doorway and closed the door behind her. "*Bischt du okay,* Ruby?"

"I just needed to rest my ankle." And her brain. And her heart.

"I thought you looked a little upset." Her mother sat on the side of the bed, so Ruby moved over a little to give her more room.

There was no putting on a brave face for Mamm. She'd raised too many *Kinner* to be fooled by a hearty denial—or even a halfhearted one. "I was—I mean, not really, but—"

"This is more than needing a little space. Your father told me that the Kuepfers have invited you home with them."

She took a deep breath. "It's very kind of them. It's also three thousand miles. Talk about space."

"A person wouldn't want to go all that way alone," Mamm said by way of agreement.

"A person wouldn't be going there alone. Under normal circumstances."

"Why would a person consider going there at all?"

Ruby snatched at a tumbling thought the way she might snatch at a sock in the dryer. "I'm not, really. Honest, Mamm, I was just interested in life on the Island and asking questions about it and the next thing I knew they were inviting me to stay."

"Something must have prompted it."

"I don't know what. Maybe they do this a lot. Who knows."

"Maybe a young man is wanting a chance with you, and he feels he'd have better success in his own district than this one."

Ruby felt at a distinct disadvantage, lying flat on her back gazing up at her mother. In her mind, she had leaped to her feet and was striding back and forth in front of the window, waving her arms as though she could push away the very thought.

"I don't know," she said feebly. "Emily asked if her brother could drive me home tomorrow night after singing." When Mamm looked the question, she answered, "I said yes."

"So he feels encouraged."

"I guess he does."

After a moment, Mamm said, "Do you like this young man well enough to encourage him?"

"I like him, sure."

"There is liking a young man, and then there's *liking* him ... in a way that leads to courting."

She turned her head away on the pillow. "At least *he* wants to court me," she mumbled.

But Mamm, for such a quiet person, had ears like a cat. "And someone else doesn't?"

Her mother's gaze, so tender and sympathetic, lay on her face like a gentle hand. Ruby turned back to meet that gaze and swallowed the lump in her throat. "In my top drawer. Unroll it and tell me what you think it means."

Mamm got up, fetched the sketch, and slipped the ribbon off it as she sat down. After a moment of gazing wordlessly at the drawing, she said, "When did he give this to you?"

For of course she knew it could only have come from one person.

"This morning, before you and Dat came down. He gave it to me and had to leave to feed the cattle. But Mamm, I don't understand it at all."

"This is a courting couple, *Liewi*."

"Is it?" The lump in Ruby's throat made it difficult to get words past it. "Or is it just best friends? Skating partners. A memory of a happy afternoon—until I fell on top of him." It suddenly occurred to her that she'd been doing a lot of falling on eligible bachelors lately. Who was next? Gideon?

"Are you sure he means skating partners? Couldn't it mean something more?"

"If it did, why didn't he just say so? Why make me guess and fret and have to ask him and then be so embarrassed I thought I'd die when he didn't answer?"

"He didn't answer?"

"*Neh. Ja.* I can't remember. We were interrupted." Mamm was still gazing at the drawing. "You really think it's a courting couple?"

"If he hadn't written that at the bottom, I would have thought so. That he was asking you in his shy, roundabout way if you wanted to court for true."

Ruby groaned. "Why can't people just say what they mean?"

"What did you say to Cale and Emily Kuepfer when they invited you to go with them?"

"I said we should talk about it some other time, when there weren't so many people around."

"And was that what you meant to say?"

"*Ja*. With half the *Gmee* in the room, it's impossible."

"It wasn't half the *Gmee*, it was only the Millers. And us. Mind you, it would be enough for church in some places." Mamm smiled at the thought. "If we get much more snow before tomorrow, we'll have a snow service here. The horses won't be able to get to Keims'."

And then she wouldn't have to ride in Cale's borrowed buggy for five miles. Would it be so bad if she prayed for more snow?

Mamm rose, rolled up and tied the drawing, and replaced it in Ruby's dresser drawer. "I don't know how to advise you, *Liewi*. It seems these two young men—"

"Three. Gideon Miller, too. I don't know what has got into them."

Mamm bit her lips, but Ruby could tell when she was smiling. The dimple denting one cheek gave her away.

"It's not funny, Mamm. I can have two for the asking, but the one I really want doesn't speak in a way I can understand. And what am I going to tell the Kuepfers?"

"It's not what these boys want, or what the Kuepfers want, or even what you want, *mei Docher*," Mamm said, her hand on the bedroom doorknob. "Ask *der Herr* what He wants. And He will send a lamp for your feet, and make the way plain before you."

Ruby subsided onto the quilt once more as the door clicked shut behind her mother. "A lamp for my feet," she said to the shadows of the pines wavering on the ceiling as the sun sank on this short Christmas afternoon. "With my luck, I'll trip over it and sprain the other ankle."

❧ 13 ❧

IT WAS ONLY through the grace of *Gott* that Zach got through the rest of the day. He couldn't go to the barn—he and baby Deborah, Rebecca and Noah, and Malena needed to stay in the house to welcome visitors until Mamm and Dat came back from the bishop's. And now here came Alden Stolzfus, banging snow off his ski boots and standing the cross-country skis next to the mud room door.

Malena's face was alight as she pulled him into the warm kitchen and plied him with savory tarts and cake ... and the Christmas fruit cookies she'd just pulled out of the oven.

"It smells *wunderbaar* in here," Alden sighed, biting into a cookie jeweled with bits of candied cherry, pear, and citron. "And you are a sight for sore eyes."

Malena made a face at him, even though her dress was the new one made for the wedding, her *Kapp* was starched to a sparkle, and Zach knew for a fact that she'd been moaning for at least two days about the snow keeping her special friend away.

Zach had to look elsewhere. Just his luck to be trapped in

his own home by not one, but two pairs of lovebirds. And here he was, the solitary crow with no prospect of a mate, despite all his efforts.

"I passed a buggy or two on the way out," Alden said as Malena curled up in her favorite chair and he sat on the floor, close enough to rest his head on her knee if he wanted to. "Joshua and Sara should be here in a little while."

"So should everyone else," Rebecca said. "Zach, was the rest of the family coming behind you?"

He shook his head. "Didn't look like it. Everyone was busy visiting and making plans when I left."

"Making plans for what?" Noah asked. "A frolic? A party? I hope it's not too soon—we're supposed to get more snow."

Zach should have kept his mouth shut. And now he had to speak into existence the idea he was trying to ignore, right here in his own living room. "There's some talk of Ruby going with the Kuepfers when they leave next week, and visiting this island of theirs."

Four pairs of eyes swung his way. In the silence, Deborah gurgled in Rebecca's lap, turning a wooden alphabet block in her chubby hands.

"Ruby Wengerd?" Malena said blankly. "Going out East? What brought this on?"

Rebecca grinned at her. "I'll give you one clue and it begins with the letter *C*."

"It can't be." Malena shook her head as though something were buzzing around her ears. "Ruby would never do something that crazy. Go all that way with no one from home? Little Joe would never allow it."

"Apparently he has," Zach said. "He was standing right there when Emily asked her parents if Ruby could go back with them."

THE AMISH COWBOY'S HOME

"But—but—" Malena's disbelieving gaze landed on Zach and he braced himself. "It's only been a week. They've only met a couple of times. That's no foundation for—for—well, for going so far away. They barely know one another."

"Better for her to go out there, if he has work," Noah pointed out. "What's he going to do here?"

"Yes, but what if she decides it's a bad idea and nothing is going to come of it? Then she's got to turn around and come back. I don't even know how far it is. The width of a whole continent."

"Three thousand miles," Zach said. "I looked it up."

"Nobody travels three thousand miles unless they're reasonably sure of what they're going for," Alden mused. "Or they see it as their only choice. Maybe *Gott* has spoken firmly to Cale and that's how he feels."

"Does he?" Rebecca caught Zach's unwilling eye. "You've spent more time with him than we have, *Bruder*. Does he plan to court her?"

"He asked Emily to ask Ruby if he could drive her home tomorrow night," he said slowly, sticking to facts and not supposition. "She said yes."

"There you have it," Noah said, nodding. "Sounds like he does plan to court her. Well, there's plenty of time to get to know a person on the train. There's literally nowhere to go and nothing to do but talk to the people you're with."

And how would Ruby survive that? Zach had a sick feeling she might handle it as badly as he had. Their family had taken the train once a few years ago to go to a wedding, and by the time they arrived in Lancaster County, Zach had almost gone around the bend. He loved his family, but other than the bunk in the sleeping compartment and the tiny restroom, he had not been able to find a single quiet space in which to collect himself and breathe. How was Ruby going to manage in the bosom of a family she'd only met a week ago?

"There are no prospects for her here in the valley," Rebecca mused. "She's run through every bachelor in the district."

"Not the Zook brothers," Malena pointed out. "They're only fifty ... ish."

"Every *eligible* bachelor," Rebecca said with mock sternness for her twin's frivolity.

This was too much for Zach. "She hasn't *run through* them. They weren't asking her out. Not the real Ruby. They were asking out the bishop's daughter. She's not stupid—she knows the difference. She gave them their chance and then said no to anything more."

Rebecca blinked at him. "And you know all this how?"

Ach, neh. He'd said too much and now both the twins were looking at him with assessment in their eyes. In another second—if he didn't distract them—they'd—

Realization broke over both their faces at the same moment, and in perfect unison they turned their heads to gape at each other.

Oh, why did he have to have twins for sisters? This was not fair.

"Why, Zachariah Miller." Malena pinned him in his seat like a raptor spotting a mouse.

Rebecca gazed at him as though he'd just turned into a completely new man right in front of her.

Zach closed his eyes and leaned his head back on the sofa cushions in defeat.

"What?" Noah said. "What did I miss?"

"*Mei Bruder* is more than just friends with Ruby," his wife informed him. "Or at least, he very much wants to be."

"That's why you ran away home instead of visiting over at

"I have twelve days. Surely in that time I can find a way to talk to her. Convince her."

"If she has feelings for you and is shy about letting them show, you won't have to convince her," Malena said in the voice of one who knows. "How can we help?"

"Hogtie Cale and lock him in the pumphouse?" Zach asked hopefully.

"Besides that."

His mind was a blank. "I don't really know yet, but when I think of something, I'll for sure and certain tell you." It all looked insurmountable from here—but the only way to start climbing a mountain was to take one step.

Outside, they heard the rattle of buggy wheels as someone emerged from the lane. Rebecca turned to look out the window. "Joshua and Sara, with Nathan. I hope they brought overnight things. I hope you did, too, Alden. Those clouds are coming in fast." She turned back to Zach. "On the sad side, it means we may not be going to Keims'. On the happy side, Ruby won't be getting a five-mile ride home."

"On the even more sad side," Alden said, "Cale can walk her home from here."

"Not with her ankle the way it is. She can barely get across a room," Zach told them. "Dat and the bishop will have us go there for church, for her sake."

"Then we'll just have to find a way to keep Cale busy." Malena's designing brain was clearly already at work. "What a shame Kate doesn't have another beautiful sister. We could ask her to distract him."

Was it too much to ask for his own sisters to be serious?

"We'll manage this, Zach," Rebecca told him, patting his knee. "Don't you worry."

It was too late to stop the avalanche of his sisters' love and desire to help.

And just as impossible not to dread what *we'll manage this* might mean.

{#}

WITH JOSHUA AND SARA AND ALDEN STAYING OVER, ZACH opened up the bunkhouse and got the stove going. The barn was divided into sections, with the bunkhouse positioned over the tack room, equipment closets, and the chickens' section, and could house up to six extra hands during the summer. Zach and Adam gave up their room to their youngest brother and his little family, then took sleeping bags and pillows over to the barn.

"Nice," Alden said, inspecting the tiny bathroom and shower. "I bet the water is cold though."

"It's heated," Zach said. "I turned it on for us."

"You missed an *Uffrohr* over at the bishop's," Adam said, dropping his toothbrush into a clean water glass by the kitchen sink. "Why did you leave so early?"

Zach was almost afraid to ask. So he answered the question instead. "With the weather coming in, I figured I'd better open up in here and get the heat going in case people were stranded over this way."

The woodstove was working already, throwing out heat that would be welcome tonight.

"What kind of uproar?" Alden asked, not even looking at Zach. "Did the bishop's pigs get out on the ice again?"

That had happened the first winter the Stolzfus family had lived in the valley. It wasn't wise to reminisce about it in Little Joe's hearing, though.

"*Neh*, nothing so fun," Adam said. "I heard some strong words out behind the barn between Cale and Gideon, though, while Dat and I were discussing leases on the other side of the wall with the bishop and his sons."

"Strong words?"

"Seems our cousin from New Mexico takes exception to Ruby's traveling so far with a family she's only known for a week. He thinks that if Ruby's going to travel anywhere this winter, it should be with Aendi Rachel's family, whom she already knows."

Zach could hardly imagine getting into a dustup anywhere near the bishop, let alone within earshot of his own barn. "And Aendi Rachel's second son, presumably, who wants to know her better."

"That was the gist of it." Adam shook his head. "The bishop was not happy with two men from away arguing over his *Docher*. He marched outside and told them that Ruby wasn't going anywhere at the moment, and if she did go, the time and the destination would be her decision, no one else's."

Alden winced and made a rueful face. "Ouch."

"*Ja*, it shut them up pretty quick. And then he left them to apologize to each other. But I didn't hear if they did. Dat figured the leases could wait for another time, and we went back inside. They should be home soon, though."

Zach gave the news about twelve hours to make its way through the district. By the time the *Gmee* met for church in small neighborhood groups, as they did during bad weather, it would be common knowledge that the Miller cousins from away were having words over the bishop's daughter, and all she had to do was choose between them.

A scenario guaranteed to make Ruby go into her closet, pull a blanket over her head, and never come out.

That evening during supper, Zach noticed that Cale and Gideon were giving each other a wide berth, sitting on opposite sides of the room to eat. Later, while Gracie, Benny, and Tobias, along with Jenny and Seth, worked on a thousand-piece puzzle set on a board on the coffee table, Gideon played with Nathan and his blocks in the living room so that Sara could eat her dinner. Maybe it was a blessing that he and Cale were both sleeping down at Daniel's—they'd be forced to shake hands and agree that they'd both been presumptuous and wrong.

Noah left Rebecca's side just on the heels of this thought, and sidled up to Zach. "If I were going to speak to a certain someone," he said in a low tone, "I'd do it while the competition is in the doghouse."

"I was going to try after church tomorrow," Zach murmured back.

"The whole herd will be there after church. If you go now, your chances are better."

Not ten minutes later, he was striding down the lane, trying to stay in the ruts the buggies had made so his feet wouldn't crunch so loudly in the frozen snow and give him away. He even had a reason to go, if anyone asked—he'd left in such an upset this afternoon that he'd forgotten his knitted scarf.

Thankfully, none of his family had brought it home with them.

The snow was falling heavily by the time he reached the county highway. He would never have made it over the shortcut—the flakes whirled in a maelstrom in his flashlight beam and made the ground a featureless blank. Maybe this hadn't been such a *gut* idea—but then, if it meant talking with Ruby, he'd brave worse.

There were still a lot of people at the Wengerd home—

augmented now by the Zook brothers, who had unaccountably decided they must pay a Christmas visit to their bishop even when it was obvious they had a fifty-fifty chance of not being able to get home again.

No one noticed Zach sidle in from the mud room or move quietly past visiting family groups. No one except Sadie Wengerd.

"*Guder owed*, Zach." She offered him a plate on which were piled toothsome squares of what looked like lemon blueberry cake, complete with lemon frosting.

He took a piece, even though he was still full from his own dinner at home. "I forgot my scarf," he said, sounding as lame as he felt. He bit into the luscious cake to cover the moment.

"It's there." She nodded toward the row of hooks in the mud room, full of coats and scarves and knitted caps. "Somewhere. Ruby found it in the room we were using for a coat room this afternoon."

"*Denki*. Is she in there?" He nodded toward the living room.

But her mother shook her head. "She came down for supper, but went back upstairs afterward. She's hurting a little bit, I think."

He tried not to let his disappointment show, and took another bite of the cake. "Could you let her know I was asking after her? I—I left kind of in a hurry. I was sorry we couldn't talk more."

"I'm sure she was, too. But you know Ruby. Even though we're practically all family, she's not completely comfortable in a crowd."

He smiled and finished the cake in one last bite. "I'm not, either. But on the other hand, when our family lives in other places, it's a gift to have them with us. I try to remember that when my cousin Seth steals the last piece of bacon at break-fast. Because he has, every morning since he got here."

Now it was Sadie's turn to smile. "You'll think of him in the future every time you take the last piece, though." The Zook brothers laughed uproariously at something Little Joe said in the other room, and Sadie's eyes became shadowed. "I'm a bit worried about those two. We can't put them up here, and no one should put a horse on the road on a night like this. But you know them—stubborn as a pair of boulders in the middle of the river. They'll try to go home, I just know it."

"We have room at the Circle M," Zach said. "We opened up the bunkhouse—Alden skiied over, and Josh and Sara made it just in time with Nathan before it started to come down hard."

"Would you ask them?" The relief shone in her eyes. "Hopefully they'll be able to make it home tomorrow after church."

Zach lost no time in making his way into the living room, only to stop dead at the bottom of the stairs.

Ruby stood on the second step, an empty glass in her hand, clearly on her way to the kitchen.

He fairly glowed with the unexpected gift of the sight of her, and held out his own hand. "Can I fill that for you?"

"*Ach, neh*—it's just water—I can—"

In less than ten seconds, he was back with the filled glass to find Ruby sitting on the step, her foot and ankle outstretched, waiting for him. The staircase was not enclosed, and led up to an open railing overlooking the great room. All the bedrooms were upstairs. As he sat beside her on the next step down, the way he often did, they could see everyone and everyone could see them. But in the happy racket of visiting family—and the Zook brothers—Zach hoped that no one would really notice them.

"You came back," she observed, after a sip of water.

"I was sorry I left so early."

"*Ischt okay* now?"

"*Ja*. I was just being stupid."

"I think Cale was the one being stupid," she said. "I heard there was a fuss out at the barn. Mamm says Dat came in looking like a thundercloud."

"A fuss—*I* heard it was an *Uffrohr*. Cale and Gideon had words over which family you were going to be traveling home with for a visit."

She snorted, then took another sip of water. "Is that what it was? Dat wouldn't tell me. *Narre*."

Zach was pretty sure the plural meant his cousins were the idiots, not her father. "He said it was your decision, and not theirs. That's what Adam told me, anyway—they were in the barn talking leases and heard the whole thing. I was at home with the twins, in case we had visitors."

"And did you?"

"*Ja*. Josh and Sara and Nathan, and Alden. Seeing him unexpectedly was Malena's Christmas present."

She smiled, acknowledging this fact. "He must have skiied."

Zach nodded. Was this the time and the place to tell her what was in his heart? But that heart, full as it was with her very presence, failed at the prospect of speaking his feelings aloud in this crowded room.

"I wish the Zook brothers had skiied," he said, losing his courage. She grinned at the picture this made in her mind, and he remembered what he'd been on his way to do when he saw her on the stairs. "Sadie wants me to convince them to come back to the Circle M. But you know them. They'll try to get home and we won't find their frozen bodies until spring."

"I'll help you." She put her glass down close to the wall, where it was less likely to be kicked over by one of the *Kinner* racing up the stairs, and held out a hand for assistance.

He offered her his arm for the two steps down, rejoicing at the small miracle that had just fallen in his lap. She gripped his forearm and he felt the warmth of her body all the way to his toes, even though only their upper arms touched. Together, they approached Hezekiah and Willard, who were trying to convince the bishop that this storm was nothing compared to the one in '86.

"Dat still remembers that one," Zach said by way of joining the conversation. "Maybe he and you can compare notes. Bring your horse over and put it in our barn, and stay the night."

Willard looked almost insulted. "What, this little flurry? Three miles of this isn't going to hurt us."

"But Mamm is worried," Ruby said in her gentle way. She hadn't let go of Zach's arm, and he saw her father notice. "If you're in the bunkhouse with the Miller boys, it will ease her heart."

"Then we'll see how it looks after church," Zach added. "That will be here, won't it, bishop?"

Little Joe nodded. "I was just telling Hezekiah that I wished we had more space. The *Kinner* are on the floor on air mattresses as it is."

"We wouldn't impose," Willard said firmly.

"Not on your folks, either," Hezekiah told Zach. "We'll be fine."

"But your horse may not be," Ruby persisted. "Remember what happened to Calvin Yoder six years ago? His horse slipped on the ice and Calvin and Dave and the horse all wound up in the ditch."

Hezekiah nodded with the memory. "Lucky that horse didn't break a leg. Can't say the same for the buggy, though. Had to get a new one, didn't they?"

"It was expensive," the bishop remembered. "Shipped it out from Pennsylvania because the nearest buggy maker had gone to a wedding and had closed the shop."

"Can you risk the horse or your buggy?" Zach asked, doing his best to look grave. "Is it really worth it when you'll be just as comfortable with us as at home?" There was no point in blandishing them with the promise of food—both of them were adventurous cooks who considered food something to be celebrated, not merely a necessity.

"Hm." Hezekiah looked at Willard. "The goats ought to be all right in the barn, but I don't know…"

Ruby chose her moment. "Please? For my mother's sake?"

Willard lost the battle first, and when he weakened, his brother clearly knew he couldn't fight on for both of them. "All right, Ruby," Hezekiah said. "Have it your way. Zach Miller, you'll ride with us?"

"I think I'll be more useful if I walk ahead of you with the flashlight," Zach said. "At least then we'll all know where the road is."

The Zook brothers got themselves into coats and boots, and made as much noise going out the door as a herd of cattle being driven into the chute. Zach collected his scarf, wound it around his neck, and pulled on his own boots. To his surprise, Ruby had followed him into the kitchen with her cane.

"Look at you," he said, fighting a pleased smile and failing.

"It's getting better," she said. "I think it's the ice—seems funny to have to use ice during the worst storm of the year so far. *Denki* for helping me convince them."

He did up the last fastener on his coat. "We make a *gut* team." And plunged in. "Like I said, we make *gut* partners."

She gazed up at him, examining his face, her brows knit in confusion. "Skating partners, maybe."

A chill traveled down his body, as if the door were open. "Not only that. In life, too. If you wanted."

Her mouth fell open. "Are you ... *proposing* to me?" Her voice went up the scale with each word until the last one came out as a squeak.

He was so shocked that words fell out of his mouth like loose rocks down a hillside. "What? Good grief. *Neh*! I only meant—I mean, not—*Neh*!"

The shock in her eyes melted into a hurt so intense he actually reached for her, as though she'd been injured. "*Ach*, I know what you meant. *Guder nacht*, Zach."

She turned and hobbled out of the kitchen, her back as straight as pain would allow.

Zach stood there, his hands loose by his sides, his head ringing just as if she had smacked him. What had just happened? What had he done to hurt her so? He had only been trying to reassure her that he wasn't going to rush her. Maybe he ought to have said that in plain words.

He had no idea how much time passed, while he stood there torn between going upstairs after her and just walking outside and sticking his head in the snow, before Sadie hurried in and said urgently, "Zach, are you going with the Zook boys? They're hitched up and heading down the lane."

He pulled himself together somehow, located his flashlight, and dimly registered that another four or five inches of snow already covered what he'd stamped down on the steps. He caught up to the Zook buggy and acted as their guide, but for a long time afterward he wondered how he'd managed the walk home. *Gott* must have taken full responsibility for their well-being, because when they finally reached the Circle M's barn, he remembered nothing of the walk down the highway, nor up their lane.

Only the frigid night. The whirling snow. And Ruby's horrified voice, saying over and over, *Are you proposing to me?*

❧ 14 ❧

IF SHE COULD HAVE SLIPPED past her parents and run after Zach, Ruby would have done it. How presumptuous could a woman be, spitting out her delighted disbelief that he was actually proposing? What idiocy had possessed her?

Because of course she'd got the answer she deserved—a *Neh* so emphatic, so shocked, that it was obvious she was so far off base that she and Zach weren't even playing in the same field.

It was her own fault. She'd become the observer instead of the participant—because that way she didn't get her feelings hurt quite so much. She tended to study people rather than talking to them. Well, obviously *der Herr* had seen it was time to teach her a lesson about that. And now, here she was, finally participating in her own life and making just as much a mess of it as ever.

What with the *Kinner* and her sisters-in-law tiptoeing noisily up and down the hallway during the night, Ruby didn't sleep much. Or maybe it was just her own brain, shouting so loudly as that scene in the kitchen with Zach played over and over, that she couldn't quiet herself enough to sleep.

Finally, when Mamm's engagement clock downstairs chimed once in its soft and elegant voice, she appealed to the One who had authored both silence and sound.

Mei Vater, hilfe mich. I've made a mess of things. Thou knowest the desire of my heart—to belong to Zach, to spend the rest of my life right here in the valley with him, among our families and the people we love and who love Thee. But our friendship may be in trouble because I presumed when I shouldn't have. Give me the words, Lord—to ask forgiveness. Give me courage—to ask for help and understanding. Help me speak—I, who spend most of the time letting others do so. I ask this of Thee, Lord, who spoke the world into existence, in the name of Thy blessed Son.

It was only when a sense of calm flowed into her tense, hurting body that she was able to fall asleep.

Sunday, December 26

At five o'clock, their usual time to rise in the morning, the first thing she did after thanking *der Herr* for the rest He had given her was to pull back the window quilt to see what was making the scraping sound outside.

"Oh my." The two words, breathed against the cold window, left a little cloud of fog.

The yard had disappeared. Or rather, there was no difference between the yard, the drive, and the lawn—it was all a featureless expanse of white, striped with gold in the lamplight, nearly to the waists of her father and her brothers. Methodically, in the pattern they used when the boys were a lot smaller than they were now, they shoveled the snow, starting at the kitchen steps and working their way to the barn, then out again across the yard. Last would be the lane, shoveling three abreast. By the time the first of the Millers arrived for church on foot, they would have a safe path the width of a buggy to walk in, even if the sides formed walls on either side.

After breakfast, there was just time to locate every possible chair in the house, the unused *Daadi Haus*, and the barn, and set them out in rows in the living room. The bench wagon, of course, had gone to the Keim place, where at least the neighbors over there would have not only the usual place to sit, but a preacher as well, since Simon Keim had that office. Meanwhile, if they ran out of chairs here, Ruby knew the *Kinner* would be just as happy to sit on the floor.

Even though Christmas had been yesterday, it wasn't really Christmas until they had concluded singing the *Loblied* and she heard her father's resonant bass as he read the words, "Where is he that is born King of the Jews? for we have seen his star in the east, and are come to worship him." He read the Christmas story, from both Matthew and Luke, and then invited some of the elders like Reuben Miller and Lorne Kuepfer to speak if the spirit so moved them.

What Ruby's family called the "snow service" progressed exactly as a regular church service, but the preaching part was shorter. And the fellowship meal began a little earlier, which was fine with Ruby since breakfast had been a good five hours ago. Throughout the service she had been careful not to look at the men's side. For one, Cale and Gideon would make far too much of it if one of them happened to catch her eye. And for two, she simply didn't have the strength to see Zach and realize again how thoroughly she had lost him.

In spite of her own embarrassment, she managed to enjoy the rich chicken and dumplings that Mamm and her sisters-in-law had made, and the leftover turkey and stuffing from Christmas dinner made fine sandwiches, layered with cranberry sauce. She could escape into the kitchen to do the dishes with her nieces, and afterward, while Cale and Gideon were distracted by the *Kinner* begging for their help to build a snow fort, she could slip up the stairs to her own room. She had no idea where Zach was—really, it was a relief not to know.

She spent the whole afternoon at her little desk, writing letters instead of visiting with the *Youngie*, as she normally would have done. Reuben and Naomi, Joshua and Sara wrapped the babies up warmly and took them home, while Tobias, Rachel, and the twins left with the elder Kuepfers around three. She could hear from all the way upstairs the Zook brothers insisting that it was time to give the roads a try, whether the county blade had come through or not. From her window, Ruby watched the little procession make its way up the lane.

A knock at her bedroom door forced her to turn away and answer it.

"Aendi Ruby," said her twelve-year-old niece, "Mammi says the *Youngie* are staying to sing, and will you come down and help with supper."

Any hope that the *Youngie* would go back to the Circle M to sing died a silent death. "*Ja*, I'll be right there. I hope some of you older ones will sing with us." When her niece looked doubtful, she bent and confided, "This isn't really a proper singing. I think it would be all right if *Kinner* under sixteen joined us. You can learn some of the songs tonight, so that when you're older, you'll already know them."

The girl skipped away to tell her siblings and cousins, and

Ruby resigned herself to having to face the music. At least she could count on keeping busy in the kitchen. Supper was leftovers and cherry pie with whipping cream poured on it, only because, as Malena said, "No one in their right mind eats ice cream in this weather, no matter how warm the stove is."

She was heartened to see the *Youngie* welcome some of the older children, finding the hymnbooks for them and sharing their handwritten songbooks. If the *Kinner* hadn't been there, they might only have filled a few of the chairs. As it was, they could all sit comfortably at the long kitchen table. Ruby made good and sure she was at the opposite end of the table from Zach, and even managed to encourage her nephews to sit across from her so that Cale and Gideon were forced to settle for places in the middle.

But no matter where she sat, she could still hear Zach's baritone under the higher voices of the *Kinner*—that sound that could make her shiver, as though someone had stroked the back of her neck with a finger. She'd been listening to him sing for nearly ten years now—since his voice had changed—and it never ceased to have this physical effect on her.

Well, she'd better get over *that*, now that she knew his little drawing had only meant "friends and skating partners," nothing more. He wasn't interested in marriage—at least, not with her.

It hurt. Her chest seemed full of pain, and every breath to sing the lines came hard, even the easy ones, like "Country Roads" and "What a Friend We Have in Jesus." Songs she'd been singing for years were an effort—as though her own breath were stifled.

Maybe the fall on the shortcut last week was finally catching up with her. Or maybe it was just grief—the loss of the hope that had kept her going for years now. *Hope deferred maketh the heart sick*. Isn't that what it said in Proverbs? Well, her heart was sick for sure and certain.

Zach clearly wasn't the one to cure it. He probably didn't even know he'd caused this wound. She had to remember that she had a way to cure it herself. Dat had already approved it. Mamm didn't need her help as much at this time of year, because there was no planting, no canning, no looking after the garden. Maybe running away from her troubles wasn't very effective, but it was a way to act. A way to leave them behind for a season, until time and distance had done their work and helped her to heal.

The prospect of not feeling this way about Zach anymore was half pain, half relief. Maybe someday it would be all relief. All she had to do was act.

All she had to do was say yes and accept the Kuepfers' invitation.

Wednesday, December 29

WITHIN A FEW DAYS OF CHRISTMAS, THE COUNTY snowplows and graders had done their good work, and Naomi was able to keep her promise to Rachel to show her around the valley a little and see what kind of work might be available for a rancher's widow.

They started close by, at the Rocking Diamond. Marina Valdez was Taylor Madison's domestic assistant ("We don't call women pursuing this career *housekeepers* anymore, Mrs Miller"), and they learned that her job combined management of the house with managing the housekeeping staff looking after the guests in the cabins ... rich *Englisch* folks who paid ten thousand a week to stay there.

Naomi saw Rachel swallow hard.

"I have a degree in hotel management," Marina explained, "as well as a good twenty years of experience in both hotels and private establishments like country clubs and estates."

"And do you like it here?" Rachel asked faintly, probably feeling as out of place in the gleaming white kitchen with its black appliances as Naomi did. Every single thing ran on electricity. What did they do when the snow took out the power lines? Start up the generators, same as the Amish did, probably.

"I do like it." Marina refreshed the cup of fancy coffee that had arrived in front of them with a fern drawn in the foam on top. "But I'm ready for a change, and with my boys going away to college in San Luis Obispo, it's time for a move. Mrs Madison is very specific in what she wants, but she communicates that well and is a fair employer. How are your computer skills?"

Rachel exchanged a helpless glance with Naomi. "Nonexistent? I can use the telephone, though. I'm a good cook, my sons tell me. Never had any complaints from the hands—though they'd have had to go without if they did. And if the farrier needed help shoeing a horse, I could do that."

Marina smiled. "It was brave of you to apply, Mrs Miller. And I don't doubt you have far more useful ranching skills than I do. But I'm afraid computer work comes with the territory—ordering supplies online, maintaining the ranch website, processing guest bookings. It's all done on this." She pulled a small tablet from an inner pocket of her black jacket, and waggled it.

There were some hills you couldn't climb, some rules you couldn't break. The *Ordnung* was very firm on the subject.

As they drove away, Rachel asked nobody in particular, "Why does a ranch need a website?"

"It's a dude ranch, *Liewi*. Not the same as a working ranch like the Circle M."

"I feel like I've spent twenty minutes on another planet. The *Kaffee* was *gut*, though. I thought the fern was a nice touch."

They passed the bishop's lane, and both of them gazed down it as far as the first turn, in case anyone was out. But there was no one—only small birds running on top of the snow banked up on either side.

"I hope Ruby's ankle is better," Naomi said. "I miss her dropping in. She and Zach are usually thick as thieves, but he hasn't left the ranch since Sunday, either." Had they had a falling out? But how could that be, when Ruby had gone up to her room and to her knowledge, hadn't spoken to Zach at all?

Or ... had he spoken and Ruby had not given him the answer he hoped for? Oh my. Naomi hoped that wasn't the case.

"Is there something going on between them?" Rachel asked. "I wish you'd tell me, because my Gideon can't take his eyes off her."

Not for worlds would Naomi break Zach's confidence. Whether he had spoken to Ruby or not, it would be up to Ruby to tell Gideon what was what if he mustered the courage to approach her.

"I'm not sure, to be honest," she said. "What I do know is that many have tried, but few are chosen. Gideon's chances are as good as ... well, as Cale's. You have to have seen the attention he's been paying her."

"I have." Rachel sniffed. "He needn't think he's so special, that Cale. He's leaving for good, and my boy will be back here by spring, if I can find a place to live and some work I can do."

Not for the first time, Naomi reminded her that the family was more than welcome to stay on the Circle M as long as they needed to.

"I have to admit," Rachel went on, "I was shocked when the Kuepfers invited her to travel home with them. Why, she's not even engaged to Cale—not that she could be, mind you. He's barely known her a week."

"I know. I was shocked, too." Goodness knew what Zach had thought of it, poor boy. "But that's Little Joe and Sadie's lookout, not ours, thank goodness."

"I suppose." Rachel sighed. "I'm in no hurry for Gideon to get serious about anyone. It's Tobias I worry about. The twins need a mother, and if he gets work as a hand on someone else's ranch..."

Naomi nodded with understanding. "It will fall to you and Susanna to mother them. At least they'll be in school, making friends. That will help."

"True. Well, no point borrowing trouble. I'll stick to my own row to hoe. Where to next?"

"The Bitterroot Dutch Café. Amish owned and Amish run. Not an electric appliance to be seen—even the cash register is one of those antique manual ones, as old as the town of Mountain Home. I'm pretty sure Ellie Bontrager will be open for the skiers."

Ellie was open, and busier than Naomi expected.

"I don't know what's got into Susan—it's been all of five days since she got engaged and she's like a different person," she said fretfully, passing two plates through the service window to her youngest *Docher*, who was only just out of

school. "Whatever happened to *obey thy father and thy mother?*
Now it's Sim says this and Sim wants that, and we hardly ever
see her."

"Rebecca says Simeon has been looking for a place to build
for some time," Naomi said mildly. "Makes sense that they'd be
looking together. Is the wedding date going to be announced
soon?"

"Your guess is as good as mine." Two more plates came out,
and since there was no one there to take them, Rachel did.
"*Denki.* Table by the window. The couple in the ski jackets."

There were a number of couples in ski jackets, but only one
pair was looking at her with hungry anticipation. Rachel
served them and topped up their coffee. She was just turning
to take it back to the kitchen when she collided with a big
man in a black Stetson. His silver bolo was shaped like a long-
horn skull, its eyes inset with turquoise. Hot coffee cascaded
down his pristine white shirt and he hollered as he jumped
back, pulling the wet fabric away from his skin.

"*Ach neh*, I'm so sorry!" Rachel looked wildly about, found
not so much as a table napkin to hand, so had to settle for
using her apron to dab at him.

The man who was waiting in a booth let out a laugh that
sounded like someone falling down a well. "Serves you right,
Brock, for getting in the lady's way."

Rachel apologized three times before Brock Madison was
able to stop both the apologies and the apron. "It's nothing,
ma'am. I've got plenty of shirts."

"If you'll let me, Mr Madison, I can launder it," Naomi
said. "I'll send one of the boys over to get it."

"Nope. Think nothing of it." His friend handed him a
couple of napkins. "You must be new here," he said to Rachel.

Ellie hustled over with a fresh white towel. "Your lunch is

on the house, Mr Madison. No, she doesn't work here. She was only trying to help." If looks could singe, Ellie's would have set Rachel's soiled, damp apron on fire.

Meekly, Rachel put the coffee pot back where she found it, and she and Naomi slunk out of the restaurant into the frigid, clear day.

"Don't tell me," Rachel said. "Mr Madison, as in the husband of Taylor Madison, as in the employer of Marina Valdez?"

"*Ja,*" Naomi said. She had backed Hester out of her spot at the hitching rail, but now her hands fell into her lap. She couldn't help herself—she laughed until she was breathless.

Poor Rachel smiled weakly. "I guess I don't get the job at either place."

"You don't *want* a job at either place." Naomi finally got hold of her dignity and guided Hester out of the parking lot, where cars outnumbered buggies today. "Ellie is a godly woman and a *gut* manager. She's a *gut* friend to those in need. But my goodness, such a temper. You're lucky it was Brock Madison you baptized. He's the only reason she was able to keep a lid on it long enough for us to get out the door."

"I feel terrible about his shirt. I hope he didn't get burned."

"With that little bit of coffee? It'll be dry by the time he leaves a tip equal to what the bill would have been. Most of it went on the floor, and I got that mopped up before Ellie even saw it."

Mountain Home was a pretty sight after the snowfall. The temperature hadn't risen enough to melt the snow into slush, and there hadn't been enough traffic to make things look dirty. A fluffy layer of snow lay on the shop roofs downtown and along the tops of the swinging, Old West signs along the neatly swept boardwalk. Despite the temperature, people were strolling along window shopping. Several shops were busy with customers, including Rose Garden Quilts.

Naomi nudged her sister-in-law. "Look. That's Malena's Christmas Present quilt in the window. I'm surprised someone hasn't bought it. She took it in the other week, before you all arrived."

"Give it time," Rachel said wisely. "That's a lovely piece of work, and it's not New Year's yet. Someone will come along wanting to spend their Christmas money."

"Better Rose and Malena have those tourist dollars than the ski hills," Naomi agreed.

They were coming up on the bridge over the unnamed creek that in many ways marked the end of the historic part of town. After this was the bar and the gas station, the bank, and Yoder's Variety Store on the left, facing a newly built structure that rumor speculated was either going to be one of those antique barns or a feed store.

"And this is the old inn I told you about. It's not for—" Naomi stopped. "Oh. Would you look at that."

A FOR SALE sign was tacked to the split rail fence that ran along the side of the wide lawn belonging to the rambling old Victorian that had once been a stagecoach stop. Two cars were parked out front.

"That white SUV belongs to the one Realtor that Mountain Home can boast of," she said to Rachel. "Looks like she's showing it. Want to go in?"

She might as well have been speaking to Hester the buggy horse.

"Rachel?"

Her sister-in-law came out of her reverie on an indrawn breath. "Can we? Can we see inside? Ach, Naomi, I didn't know you meant this place in your letter. I saw it on the trip in from the train and it broke my heart. It's so *lonely*."

Naomi closed her mouth firmly on the words, *Not any more.*

She flapped the reins over Hester's back and urged her over the bridge, then turned left down the road that paralleled the creek. A much smaller bridge spanned it here and led into the recently shoveled parking lot. Hester wasn't fond of bridges, mostly because of the change in sound under her hooves. This one would need to be fixed up, too, before it broke and dropped a supply truck into the water.

Alden's new gate was open. A sign hung from a piece of wire, probably the same way it had for fifty years. Or a hundred and fifty.

Tumbleweed's Refuge.

Not the most appealing name, Naomi had always thought, for an inn. But if you were the only game in town back at the turn of the century, it probably didn't matter. She opened her mouth to say so to Rachel as she brought Hester to a stop beside the Realtor's SUV.

But her sister-in-law was already out of the buggy, and heading toward the front porch as though she were running for a train.

15

NEW YEAR'S EVE

Friday, December 31

TWO NIGHTS LATER, over a big family dinner of chicken noodle casserole, squash pie, and slow-roasted beef ribs, Zach was astounded to learn about what had been going on in their expanded household while he'd been out riding fence in the snow and moping about the sorry state of his life. He hadn't seen his aunt so happy in all the years since Onkel Marlon had passed away.

"I can hardly believe this might be real." Aendi Rachel's eyes sparkled. She looked ready to jump out of her skin. Mamm had to nudge her to remind her to eat.

"What's going on?" Adam asked. "Gid and Seth have been out on the range with us, and we haven't seen much of you."

"I think it's more than just you working," Mamm told them. "Aendi Rachel has been wheeling and dealing and we haven't been home much. Why don't you tell them, Rachel?"

"I don't know if I can be coherent enough," their aunt said, clearly making an effort to pull herself together. "Boys—on

Wednesday, I fell in love, and today I've made a commitment. I suppose that's the easiest way to explain it."

Total silence from everybody under the age of forty met this astounding statement.

"Aendi Rachel, are you engaged?" Malena asked faintly. "Even for this family, that seems—"

"—quick," Rebecca finished.

"It depends on what you're committing to," Dat said, unable to keep a straight face. "On Wednesday, your aunt got her first look at Tumbleweed's Refuge." At the puzzled looks around the table, he added, "That rundown inn by the creek in town." To Malena, he said, "Alden made a gate for it this past autumn."

"Ah," she said, the light going on. Clearly his sister had never given the poor old inn more than a passing glance in her life. Not that Zach had, either.

"It's not run down," Aendi Rachel protested. "If you were a hundred and some-odd years old, Reuben Miller, you'd need some TLC, too. I'm prepared to give it that."

"Wait—" Gideon looked as though someone had pulled the rug out from under him and then sideswiped him with it. "Back up. You bought a what now?"

"For true?" Zach asked. "Dat, you really think this is wise?"

But Rachel answered him. "Yesterday we went over to see your neighbor next door, and between him and the Realtor, and Reuben's sharp eye for detail, we negotiated with the seller to what I feel was as reasonable a price as I was going to get. I don't know what it's been in the past," Aendi Rachel went on firmly, "but from here on out, the tumbleweeds are going to have to find refuge somewhere else. It's going to be a bed-and-breakfast called the Wild Rose Amish Inn. I wasn't sure about putting the word *Amish* on the sign, but Mr. Madison assured me that it was a selling point, and that people would find it more easily."

"But ... Brock Madison?" Rebecca sounded confused. "How does he come to be in our family's business?"

Zach wondered that, too. Give Brock and Taylor Madison an inch, and they'd take a mile. Look at how they'd treated Sara over her hay farm.

Dad nodded at the validity of the question, as if he remembered the hay farm, too. "The thing is, Brock Madison is a force in this valley. Not only did the seller's Realtor agree to practically anything he asked, I felt that of our *Englisch* acquaintances, he has the most helpful experience in buying and selling land."

"And," Mamm said, "if Brock Madison feels he's invested in it, even if it's not a cash investment, he's very likely to send business Rachel's way. He wouldn't want to look as though he gave advice on a business that wasn't successful."

Zach sat back in his chair, feeling a little winded. He shouldn't be amazed at how well Mamm read people. He could absolutely see this pattern in Brock Madison's behavior over the years. If the man believed that something was a reflection on him, he would go to the ends of the earth to make sure that reflection was favorable. Maybe not just for himself, but at the very least for the valley where he'd chosen to live, and the people he called his friends.

Zach supposed that they were lucky the *Englisch mann* considered Dat a friend.

"So what now?" Tobias asked. "Did you actually close with the seller? Or did you just make an offer?"

Mamm said, "There were people looking at the place when Rachel and I first got there."

"They dropped out," Rachel told her *Kinner*. "I have absolutely nothing to base this on, but I think Mr. Madison's involvement might've frightened them off, thinking that the price would rise instead of drop."

"So, what happens to us now?" Seth wanted to know. "When are we going to move? What about the horses? And the rest of the stock?"

"We have to talk about that, *mei Sohn*," she said. "But for now, all I know is that the seller has accepted my offer, contingent on our ability to sell the ranch."

"We're not leaving until Thursday," Tobias said. "Isn't all this a little hasty?" His grey eyes, which seemed sad most of the time unless he was looking at his children, were downright worried now.

"Sometimes the only difference between a dream and a plan is the fact that you're ready when opportunity knocks," his mother said. "I came here with the intent of finding respectable work for me and Susanna, while you boys were signing on as hands at other ranches. I never dreamed of innkeeping." She gave a helpless little laugh. "I don't know a thing about it."

"It can't be much different from board and room for the hands," Susanna suggested.

"Your way of doing it will be different from Taylor Madison's way, I'll guarantee you that," Dat put in.

"The place is livable," Rachel said, "but your *Onkel* has suggested some renovations, like stripping back the walls to put in *gut* insulation and installing new woodstoves so I can welcome guests during all four seasons. At the moment, it's only a high-season place. The rest of the year, the seller closed it up. It's going to take a lot of work, and I'm going to need all of your help so that it's possible for us to open on the first day of fishing season next year."

Zach ran over the calendar in his mind. Some dates were important, and that was one of them. "The third Saturday in May. Like you folks, outside of maintenance and repairs, in the winter we're not up on the allotments, and not giving cattle their shots or branding them or hauling them anywhere."

Adam nodded. "We could pitch in and lend a hand—at least, until it was time to get ready for shots and branding, and then spring turnout."

The warmth of Aendi Rachel's gratitude was like a sunbeam. "I surely do appreciate that, boys. I would never want to take you away from your work here, but I'll take whatever hours you can spare." She laid her knife and fork carefully in the middle of her plate. "For now, my next question is for my own boys and you, Susanna. I know we had originally planned to stay until the day after Old Christmas, same as the Kuepfers here. If you *Youngie* wanted to stay longer, I was prepared to presume on my brother-in-law's hospitality and do that.

"Now, I feel I should go home as soon as I can. As soon as I can rebook the train tickets. I want to track down the man who managed the sale of the ranch to your father and me all those years ago."

"I don't think he's in the business anymore, Mamm, but his son is," Tobias said. "He has an office in his house in Chama. Which I only know because one of his clients has a grazing lease with the outfit next door, and we were all talking one day."

"*Gut.* I'll tell him that I want the ranch put on the market. Reuben agrees that the price I have in mind is fair—the same price we talked about over a year ago, Tobias. While it's waiting for a buyer, we can be packing up, doing a proper church cleaning in barns and house, and generally getting ready to move out."

"Don't you have to clear all this with your bishop?" Lorne Kuepfer asked. "When one of our families moves to a new district, both bishops correspond and make sure they're a *gut* fit for the community."

"We'll tell him as soon as we get home," Gideon said.

Tobias added, "The bishops here correspond in the same way. But when ours hears the news, I wouldn't be surprised if we all pull out of the valley at the same time. He was only waiting for us, Lorne."

"I'd better add that to my list," Rachel said, looking as though she wanted a piece of paper and a pencil. "Talk to Little Joe."

"He'll welcome the news," Reuben said. "I can do that, if you like."

"Or I can," Cale said.

"No, I should," Gideon said firmly.

Reuben's gaze moved from one eager face to another. Zach knew he wasn't fooled for a second—the bishop wasn't the attraction. Ruby was.

Under his Onkel's silent regard, Gideon gulped. "Of course you're the right person to do it, Onkel. Standing in the place of our father."

Dat nodded in approval.

"Mamm, my goodness," Susanna said a little breathlessly, as though she hadn't picked up on Dat's brand of silent discipline at all. "I feel like I've been picked up by a tornado and I don't know where it's going to put me down."

"I'm sorry not to talk all this over with you, *mei Kinner*. But I had to strike while the irons were hot." She was silent a moment, as though choosing her next words. "I pray that *Gott* will direct the right buyer to our dear old place. Because I believe He has made the way plain for us to come here. The old life will pass away, and all things will be made new. Including that old inn."

"Your timing is perfect," Cale said with a grin. "The *Englisch* calendar over there on the wall says tonight is New Year's Eve."

Amid the laughter, Zach had to admire his aunt's courage. This was not the kind of talk he was used to hearing from his relatives. The Millers were a pretty cautious bunch, given to taking their time over decisions, and planning carefully in order to make sure that everything was done according to the Lord's will, their own needs and desires taken into account, but definitely coming in second.

It was a *gut* example to follow, especially where love was concerned. There, a person was well advised to wait upon the Lord for as long as it took to find the right partner. There could be no moving forward without *Gott* setting the lamp to your feet first. Was that his problem? Had he not spent enough time before *der Herr*, asking for the way to be made plain? Or had he just allowed his feelings for Ruby to grow to the point that he took it for granted the Lord approved?

Maybe he'd better check himself and get his priorities straight. Because he was certainly not doing very well on his own.

"We'll all go home with you, Mamm," Tobias said at last, interrupting Zach's train of thought. "There's no point in holding things up. Once the ranch sells, we should be ready to come back and start work—no dawdling."

"You'll stay with us when you do, of course," Dat said. "You could probably camp at the Tumble—I mean, at the Wild Rose Amish Inn, but it might be more efficient if the whole place is turned over to the carpenters as a work site. Best to live here."

"I agree," Mamm said. "Each night over supper, we can talk about what needs to be done the next day. You'll need to order in supplies from Libby. That will take time." She glanced at Noah. "Our new son here is a carpenter by trade. What do you think about him acting as foreman?"

Noah's slow smile showed how pleased he was at not having to push himself forward and outright ask for the job. "I'd be happy to," he said. "At the moment my brother and I have nothing major on the books. I couldn't volunteer my time, though. I've got *mei Fraa* to support and a home to save up for." His gaze rested lovingly on Rebecca's face, his delight visible at using the words *my wife* in public. "But I'd give you the family discount."

Rachel smiled back. "My kind of terms."

Tuesday, January 4

THE AMISH DID NOT PAY MUCH ATTENTION TO THE *Englisch* New Year's traditions—for them, the new year was more of a spiritual beginning, with its first day having been the previous Sunday and the preaching that focused on the birth of Christ. Any attention the date got was only because of the inconvenience of the train offices being closed for the holidays. So, it wasn't until the following Tuesday that the *Englisch* taxi-van came to take the New Mexico Millers to Libby. They would overnight in the same bed-and-breakfast inn where Reuben, Rebecca, and Noah had stayed at Easter while Naomi had been in the hospital for little Deborah's birth. The train left at five the next morning.

"You might see what tips the young woman who runs the B and B can pass on to you," Reuben suggested as Rachel fastened her coat. "She seems to enjoy her work."

"And the food was really *gut*," Rebecca added, wrapping her arms around her aunt in a hug. "Safe travels, and we'll hope to see you again very soon."

The taxi-van trundled away down the lane. After it made the right turn on to the county highway, the sun glinted off its windows like a final farewell as it sped toward Mountain Home.

HER COAT AND SNOW BOOTS ON, A BOWL OF SCRAPS IN ONE hand, Ruby opened the kitchen door with the other to find Cale Kuepfer on the back porch.

"Goodness! You startled me." She adjusted the bowl on her hip and closed the door behind her. "*Wie geht's*, Cale?"

"They're all well up at the ranch." He fell into step beside her. "Are those for pigs or chickens?"

"Chickens. After the ice debacle, we don't keep pigs anymore."

"Somebody mentioned that the other day. What happened?"

With the passing of time, she'd learned to smile at the memory of that day, not flinch. Dat, sadly, had not yet reached that point. "We had about a dozen pigs, and one year we had a really cold snap just before butchering time. It was late October—weeks before we usually get a hard freeze. Anyway, the creek froze—not enough so you could walk out to the middle, but enough so you could skate along the edges near the banks. Those pigs got out somehow and before anyone realized it, they were all slipping and sliding on the ice, and—"

"Don't tell me." Cale covered his face as though he couldn't bear what was coming next.

"*Ja*, exactly. A couple of them went through, and by the time we got out there, they'd drowned."

"Did you butcher them anyway?"

"First we had to catch the others, and I'll leave to your imagination the spectacle of my father chasing those pigs on ice. We butchered the drowned ones anyway. It was enough to cure you of liking pork, for a few months, at least. Anyhow, we've never kept pigs since."

"Did you learn how they got out?"

"Pigs are smart. Dat figures they got a nose under the gate latch and wiggled it loose, because no one would have opened that gate and simply walked away."

She could tell he was smothering laughter, until finally it just busted loose. He had to stop walking and wipe tears from his eyes. "I'm sorry," he gasped. "But the bishop—"

She couldn't help grinning, too. "He says *Gott* will use any means at hand to keep His people *deemiedich*—including inspiring pigs to a jailbreak."

That set Cale off again, and even when she went into the chicken coop and distributed the leftover oatmeal and carrot peels to the hens, she heard him outside chuckling like an owl.

Her bowl empty, she closed and latched the door. He fell in beside her again for the walk back to the house, and she had to ask. "So, what is your errand today? What's happening at the Circle M?"

"Our numbers are down. Rachel and her family have gone."

"Gone!" She stopped in the yard between barn and house.

"But they weren't supposed to leave until Friday. Ach, Mamm will be disappointed she didn't get to say good-bye to Rachel."

By the time he was finished telling her all about the Wild Rose Amish Inn and the changes that *der Herr* was making in that family's lives, she was breathless with astonishment. "My goodness. Reuben was over here the other night talking to Dat, but he never said a word to us."

"Maybe Reuben asked him not to," Cale pointed out. "If the ranch doesn't sell, it all comes to nothing."

What else was going to come to nothing, if Ruby didn't act? As Mamm was fond of saying, when *Gott* put an opportunity in your path, you were either ready to take it or you dillydallied until you missed it. Ruby had been waiting for Zach to speak for how many years now? And here was Cale, interested and willing to see where things might go, if only they had time to spend together.

Zach didn't want to marry her. He'd said so.

Many a woman had settled for second best and been happy.

Maybe it wasn't exactly second best if she gave Cale a chance. Maybe *Gott* had inspired Emily with the idea to travel home with them to put this opportunity in front of Ruby. The question was, did she have the courage to take it?

"I've been thinking," she said. No more words came out. She was climbing the steps of the back porch, but she felt as though she were standing on the edge of a cliff, looking at a pool of water far below whose depths she couldn't measure.

"I'm listening," Cale said. He leaned on the post, giving her all the time in the world.

"You're still leaving, aren't you?"

"As far as I know. Unless Mamm and Dat fall in love with a

run-down inn or some ranch at the back of beyond, our tickets are still good for Friday."

"Well..." *Jump.* "I was thinking that maybe ..." *The water is deep enough. It won't kill you. And if you have to swim back to shore, you still can.* "I'd like to accept your family's offer, if it's still open."

She forced air into her constricted lungs, as though she'd surfaced from a deep plunge.

Incredulous joy filled Cale's face. "Seriously, Ruby? You want to come with us on Friday, back to the Island?"

Breathing was getting easier. "*Ja*, I would. I've never been farther than Wyoming. The Millers go to Whinburg Township, but I never have, even though Dat has relatives there. It —it will be an adventure."

He grabbed her and swung her in a circle, forcing all the hard-earned air out of her lungs. "I'm so happy! Emily will be over the moon. What? Oh, sorry."

Her squeaks of protest had penetrated and he put her down.

"Can you just check with your parents?" she managed. "Make sure it's still all right?"

"I can guarantee it will be all right, but *ja*, I'll check. And if you want, I'll ask Dat to call the train people and book tickets for you. Do you have a map? I can show you our route."

Mamm found them in Dat's office, poring over the big map of the United States that Dat had pinned to the wall. She looked over their shoulders as Cale's finger traced the route through Chicago to Detroit to Montreal to somewhere called Moncton, New Brunswick. Beyond it, Prince Edward Island lay in the Atlantic, shaped like a slice of cake or a tri-tip roast.

"So you've decided to go, have you?" she asked Ruby.

"Cale needs to check that the offer is still open, but ... *ja*.

I've decided." Her voice was quiet, partly because she could see a million questions in Mamm's eyes and she didn't want a single one to come out in front of Cale.

But Mamm only nodded. "If you're leaving Friday, you'll spend that night in Libby."

"That's what Rachel and her family did this afternoon," Cale said. "This business with her buying the inn put the whole house into a flap over the weekend. It's a wonder the right people got into the taxi-van and half didn't get left behind."

"Did you know about that, Mamm?" Ruby asked. "About Tumbleweed's Refuge?"

Mamm nodded. "But it wasn't for me to spread further. Well, *Docher*, we have a few days yet. We'll need to look out the small suitcase and see how full you can get it. You'll want to pack some food, too." She sighed, and gripped Ruby's shoulder. "Old Christmas will be a farewell dinner this year. It'll take me a little minute to get used to all these changes."

If you only knew, Ruby thought. She would be saying farewell to a lot more than her own family. If this path led where she thought it might, she'd be saying good-bye to the Millers as well. Probably for good.

16

AFTER SOME SHUFFLING of people and chairs, the Circle M family and the Kuepfer family rearranged themselves around the big kitchen table that evening, with only a smaller table pushed up on one end to accommodate the overflow. The younger Kuepfers seemed happy to take that over, as far from their parents' eyes as possible.

Salome Kuepfer passed the bowl of mashed potatoes and the gravy boat to Emily. Zach took the big platter from Cale and dished himself a good helping of what Mamm called "finger steaks"—deep fried venison strips. Squash casserole and a spicy coleslaw, pickles, and hot biscuits melting with butter completed the meal.

"Well," Salome said, "it looks like our traveling party may increase by one. Cale tells me that Ruby Wengerd has decided to come along after all."

Zach's stomach plunged, his fingers turned to rubber, and his knife and fork clattered to his plate. Thank goodness he'd just passed the platter. "When did this happen?"

"I went over there after Rachel's family left," Cale said. "I thought I'd let Ruby know that they'd headed out."

"That was kind of you," Mamm said. Her glance flicked to Zach, but she said nothing more.

"Ruby is going to Prince Edward Island with you?" Malena asked, as if she hadn't heard correctly. "Leaving on Friday? This Friday?"

Emily nodded, her smile wide and sincere. "Isn't it exciting? I'm looking forward to sharing the trip with her—Cale says she's never been farther than Wyoming."

Cale began to recite the major stops along the train route, but Zach's mind seemed to have congealed in sheer horror. When Adam nudged him and asked him what had happened to his appetite, he picked up his silverware and ate automatically, tasting nothing.

This was what it all had come to? He had been cudgeling his brain for days, trying to think of a way to ask her not to go, to tell her his feelings for her. The whole time, he'd had this horrible feeling that she was slipping away—that every day that passed was a day she receded farther out of his reach.

Those feelings, at least, hadn't been wrong.

She's made her choice, cowboy. Give it up and let her go.

But he couldn't. Yes, he'd been clumsy and hadn't been able to express himself properly. It was no surprise that he, who hardly talked at all in the course of a day, except maybe to Bachelor Buttons the horse or to the cattle, couldn't get a sentence out that would make sense to a woman. But surely this wasn't the end?

Wasn't there some way he could stop her?

Not if she's chosen Cale. That's a pretty big statement—traveling across the whole continent to get to know a man. Shows her intentions.

Yes, it did, but ... usually people waited until they were

married to do things like that. Emily—maybe prompted by Cale, the brother she loved, maybe not—had arranged it so the invitation had come from the family in the first place, not from the eldest son. Ruby would be going as Emily's friend, not Cale's future fiancée. All very innocent and above board, or the bishop would never have agreed to it.

Zach could see the inevitable conclusion now, sometime in the early spring. A letter would arrive announcing their engagement, and he would lose his only chance at love and a home of his own.

If he hadn't been sitting at the dinner table surrounded by talking, laughing people, he would have let the lump in his throat turn into a full-blown pity party.

As it was, he found his mother's gaze resting on him more often than was comfortable. And when he shoveled down the rice pudding for dessert without really registering it, her eyes seemed to fill with dismay.

He disliked rice pudding almost as much as Ruby disliked potato salad.

After dinner, thank goodness, there were barn chores to do. And somehow, after buttoning up the chickens' side of the barn, Rebecca and Malena tracked him back to the bunkhouse, where a man ought to have been safe from pursuit.

"Goodness, it's freezing up here. Who let the stove go out? Zach, I can see what you think of this Prince Edward Island plan," Malena said, getting down to business. "I thought you were going to break down at supper."

"I don't think anyone outside the family noticed, though," Rebecca assured him. "I can't believe she'll go through with it, Zach. She barely knows them—and as for Cale, he's not the man for her at all."

"I can't believe that all our tricks and ambushes since

THE AMISH COWBOY'S HOME

Christmas did no good at all," Malena complained. "We thought we were so smart, keeping Cale out of the way, giving you opportunities to be with Ruby, and all for nothing."

"It's not your fault," he sighed. "I've come up with a thousand ways to talk to her, and not one got off the ground—partly because it took so long to repair all the west fences after the storm, and partly because I'm losing it. I'm at my wits' end, and only three days left."

"You could draw her another picture," Rebecca suggested.

But he shook his head. "I thought I was being as obvious as could be with the last one. But she thought I meant skating partners, not life partners."

"Did you explain to her what you really meant?" Malena sounded skeptical.

"I tried! And then she thought I was proposing right there in the mud room, and ... argh." He sat on the bunk, which had only a bare mattress now that he and Adam were back in their room, and lowered his head into his hands. "What is wrong with me that I can't just come out and say, *Can I court you? Can we be special friends?*"

"You could write a letter," Rebecca suggested. "Say what you feel, in black and white."

"I'm not Adam," he groaned.

His sisters looked at each other, and between them flashed one of those voiceless messages that never meant any good to hapless brothers standing in the way.

"Instead of sitting up here moaning," Malena told him, "march over there right now and tell her. Beg her not to go, if you have to. Just do it."

He tried to speak, but his throat closed. He tried again. "Words just get messed up when I say them. It never used to be that way with her—we'd talk all day if someone let us. I don't know what happened."

"It's harder when it means the rest of your life," Malena said soberly. "Have you taken it to *der Herr*?"

He nodded. "*Pray without ceasing* has pretty much been my second job the last couple of days. Buttons figured out early on that I wasn't talking to him. The cows weren't so sure."

Rebecca was frowning at the glimpse of the half moon rising over the trees. "Words may not do any good, and pictures didn't. What's left?"

"A grand romantic gesture, like bidding nearly two thousand dollars on a quilt?" Malena quipped.

"That might have worked for you," her twin informed her, "but what can Zach do?"

"Outside of building a house or buying a buggy for her, I don't know." Malena sighed. "What if you—"

And suddenly, as if a bell had rung deep inside him, Zach knew. "That's it."

"You're going to buy her a horse?" Rebecca looked aghast. "That will cost a sight more than even Malena's quilt."

"*Neh.*" Zach could hardly breathe. "Dat says he's willing to give me a parcel of land on the point beyond Daniel's place—where that copse of aspens is. What if I built the house for her on paper?"

His sisters stared at him.

"I've done it a dozen times in my mind—elevations, rooms, square footage. What if I drew a home for her? *Our* home?"

"Zach, you're not even dating," Rebecca reminded him gently. "Wouldn't it be better to start with a ride in the buggy somewhere? Take her to the Bitterroot Dutch Café for breakfast in the morning."

"No time," Malena said. "There's only tomorrow and

Thursday, and then they leave. I'm telling you, it's got to be the grand gesture. I think drawing the house and showing her his dreams of the future is a *gut* idea."

"And what if she turns me down flat, like she did last time?" Zach said miserably.

"You surprised her," Rebecca said. "And I have to agree with Malena. You've got no time to lose. It's the grand gesture or nothing. Make it *gut, mei Bruder*. Make it *gut*."

When Zach got back to the house, their families were in the living room, talking over the events of the day and going over the route the train would take, even the younger ones describing the stops and what the land looked like. Nobody seemed to notice when Zach loped upstairs to his and Adam's room, where he lit the lamp and took out his sketchbook, his soft and hard lead pencils, and his box of colored pencils. Organizing them on the desk calmed him.

He could see the house in his mind, though of course when they actually got down to drawing up plans, Ruby's opinions and thoughts would come first. Hadn't he and Ruby talked about this very thing? Only then, it had been about Adam's house. This would be the first idea, a point in time, as she'd said, not the final product.

He visualized the house, sitting on the high point of land where the aspens shivered in the autumn sunlight. The yellow pencil—the green—white for the trunks. The house in front of them, freshly finished, the colors of warm wood a contrast with the sparkling river below. A row of tall windows that let light and scenery into the living room where the *Gmee* would come for church. And a hint of its length and depth, where kitchen and bedrooms would be.

Callouts, that's what he would do. She couldn't see inside unless he did smaller drawings showing the layouts of the rooms. *Ruby's sewing room. Zach and Ruby's room. Nursery. Kitchen.*

He turned to a fresh sheet of clean white paper and picked up his trusty No. 2 pencil.

Adam came in a couple of hours later, glanced at what he was working on, and got into bed without trying to talk. He was used to Zach not answering when he was deep in the creation of a picture—when the world under his pencil was almost more real than the world in which his brother might want to say *guder nacht*.

Zach didn't stay up all night. When he did go to bed, he fell asleep with the drawing still alive in his mind. In dreams, he moved through it, making note of what he'd call out here or there. The next morning, Zach did his chores in a daze, ate breakfast without speaking, and went back upstairs to work.

All he had was today. Ruby would be busy tomorrow with her family, and then gone Friday. It was now or never.

Wednesday, January 5

AROUND MIDAFTERNOON, NAOMI'S WORRIED MIND GOT THE better of her. She'd been arguing with herself since breakfast. Zach was twenty-six. A man. He did not need his mother putting her oar in and trying to steer his canoe. But at the same time, that helping of rice pudding last night had tattled on him. If he didn't even realize what he was putting in his mouth, his mind was occupied by something so important that small details like a dessert he never ate meant nothing.

So when he went upstairs and didn't come down again, not even for lunch, Naomi made up her mind.

The door wasn't closed, so she felt it would be all right to go in. He was bent over a picture, she could see that instantly. It must be a very important one for him to lose track of the world around him to this degree. She didn't think he was even aware of her as she stopped behind him and looked over his shoulder.

She drew a long breath as she recognized the location—the point out past Daniel's that fell away to the river meadow. The copse of golden aspens, their leaves like an unexpected handful of treasure amid the solemn pines. And the house. Oh, just look at the house!

Zach's talent for drawing was a gift from *Gott*. Her *Daadi* had had the same, but in those days, with a young family to feed, there had been no time for drawing, or money for pencils and paper unless they were used at school. She had only seen one of his pictures in her life, hidden away in her mother's cedar chest. And when Sharon Glick had passed away, the other relatives must have cleared out the chest, because she never knew what became of it. She remembered it vividly, though. Horses, nodding over the rail of a fence. Forty years later, she could still see them, each one drawn in such detail its eyes practically spoke.

Now, the home that Zach dreamed of building for Ruby— for this had to be a gift for her, with all these hours put into it —sat contentedly among the trees. Half a dozen circles surrounded it on the paper, like the callouts that had been on the plans for this very house, showing details. But these weren't plumbing and heating ducts. They were like miniatures, looking down into furnished rooms. *Ruby's sewing room* was written next to one in orderly capitals. It showed a worktable, a chair drawn up in front of the treadle Singer, a cabinet with its doors open opposite, clearly meant for fabric. All as a sparrow perched on the Coleman lamp hanging from the ceiling might see them.

Gently, she laid a hand on his shoulder.

He jumped, clearing the hard seat of the chair by an inch, she was sure. "Mamm! You startled me."

One hand made as if to cover the drawing, then he caught it back.

"This is *wunderbaar, mei Sohn*," she breathed. "If this doesn't make her change her mind and stay, I don't know what will."

"Do you think so?" His eyes broke her heart. The eyes of someone making a last-ditch effort, and who was far from certain of success.

"You've had no chance to talk at all since last church Sunday?"

He shook his head. "The storm busted up the west fences, and by the time Adam and I got them all fixed, a week had disappeared. I'm out of daylight where she's concerned. I want to go over tonight." He swallowed, and touched the paper. "But with my luck, Cale or Emily will decide they have to help her with packing or some such, and I won't get my opportunity."

All her vows to stay out of it were swept away on a surge of love.

"You leave Cale and the others to me and your brothers and sisters. You should go over while we're clearing up after supper. Lots of busyness, lots of noise. They'll think you're slipping out to do chores."

Zach gazed at her. "You really want me to court her, don't you?"

"I do," she said baldly. "She's like a daughter to me as it is. Nothing would make your father and me happier than to see her in this beautiful house." She glanced at the drawing. "No one wants her to go all the way across the continent, Zach. Not even for a harmless visit."

"Except Cale and maybe Emily."

"And maybe Ruby herself, if she thinks you don't care. Is that it?" When he didn't reply, she pressed softly. "How did she come to think that?"

He hunched in his chair as though he could make his tall, lanky self smaller. "I messed up. She didn't understand what I meant with my drawing of the skaters and when I tried to tell her, she thought I was proposing. I wanted her to know I'd give her all the time she needed, so I said *neh*, I wasn't, not at all—"

"Oh dear."

He seemed to deflate even further. "Words are not my friends, Mamm. Most of the time, talking isn't even my friend. Except with Ruby."

The picture he had drawn filled her mind with the wonder of the future. "I think this picture is worth ten thousand words. A million. You show her this, and you show her your hopes. Your dreams. Your heart."

His bottom lip trembled, just a little, and he blinked once or twice very fast.

Naomi hugged him from behind. Her second son, so quiet, so undemanding. Always doing what was asked of him. Easy to overlook if he were in the same room as Daniel or Malena. But all the same, the ranch wouldn't function without him. Without his loving care, his attention to detail, his work ethic … all things reflected in this very picture.

"Right after supper," she repeated softly, and kissed his cheek. "Show her this, and let your heart speak. Hers will reply. I know it."

❦ 17 ❦

BY THE TIME supper was to go on the table, Zach was nearly coming out of his skin with tension. How many more times did the minute hand on the clock have to creep around its face before he could walk over to the bishop's?

He had to find something to do with himself, so he went down to the basement to tend the woodstove. He had a couple of chunks of oak nicely piled and the flames just beginning to catch, when Cale moseyed down the stairs.

Was the man following him? If he wanted to talk about Ruby, or how *wunderbaar* the trip was going to be, he'd find himself talking to the stove instead.

"Need some help?"

Zach shrugged. "I was just going to clean up the woodpile. Stack it a bit neater."

He didn't want the help. If the job were done any faster, he'd be stuck staring at the clock again. But if a person offered to help, and you turned them down, Mamm had taught them long ago, it wasn't likely they'd make the offer again. And you might need their help worse some day.

"I need something to do," Cale said, following Zach's lead with the stacking pattern. "If I don't, I'll go over and bother Ruby, and her father probably wouldn't appreciate that."

"She's not one for company if she's busy," Zach allowed. "With Old Christmas tomorrow, they're probably cooking and baking up a storm. Just like here. My sisters have roped Emily and Jenny into helping them make shortbread."

"I know. I've been tossing wood, and I think my brothers are cleaning tack."

Mamm had been true to her word. So what was Cale doing down here, then?

"It's just that I don't know if Ruby's coming home with us for herself, for my sister's sake ... or for me."

Zach buttoned his lips on the words that wanted to spill out and fly around the basement like blue jays with needle-sharp beaks. "I hear she wants to see a bit of the country." That was noncommittal enough, wasn't it?

"I know she's becoming friends with my sister. It's hard not to like Emily. I don't know what's wrong with that yahoo who was courting her."

"Maybe Emily figured out he was a yahoo."

His unwelcome companion chuckled. "But Ruby is hard to read. She's nice to everybody. I can't tell if her being nice to me is because she likes me—or because she likes me as well as the dog or the horses."

Ruby? Hard to read? Well, maybe if you hadn't known her all your life. "It's a *gut* start, I guess," he ventured.

"Something to build on," Cale said, apparently agreeing with something Zach hadn't said. He was almost to the middle of the pile. Zach hoped he'd finish, go back out to the barn, and leave him alone with the stove and his thoughts. "I do have feelings for her. I just don't know how soon to show them. I don't want to scare her off before we even get to Denver."

"I don't think that's something you can schedule," Zach said, trying to recover from Cale's blunt confession. "It's supposed to come naturally, isn't it?" Listen to him, spouting wisdom like he hadn't scared Ruby off himself already. Like he wasn't about to plunge into a last-minute attempt to woo her back.

"I guess it is. Do you think I have a chance, Zach? I really like her. I just don't know if she likes me in the same way."

Now, why had *der Herr* put him in this position? Him, of all people? *What am I supposed to say, Lord?*

He was no judge of people's emotions, but it looked to him as if Cale meant what he said. "Really liking" someone was in a different league altogether from liking your dog or your horse. And here was his whole family doing what they could to get everyone out of the way so that Zach could have his chance. What had he started? Was this the act of a brother—of a Christian man—to give his cousin the runaround so that he could try to take what Cale wanted?

Oh, he'd got himself into a tangle, for sure and certain.

"Zach?" Cale glanced at him. "You're not saying anything. Does that mean you don't think I have a chance?"

In the silence, a line of Scripture Dat that had quoted during church sounded in his memory: *And ye shall know the truth, and the truth shall make you free.*

He knew the truth. But Cale did not. Zach was in bondage to his own actions, and so was his family. If he didn't speak, it would only get worse. That was no way to treat his cousin, to say nothing of his brother in Christ.

"Cale, I haven't been honest with you."

If his cousin had been trying to smile, it completely failed now. "She doesn't like me," he said flatly. "That's what you're telling me? And she just doesn't know to say it?"

Zach shook his head. "I don't know how Ruby feels. I only know how I feel." He dragged in a breath. "I've been in love with her half my life. If she goes away and doesn't come back, I —I don't know what I'll do."

Silence. The wood popped in the stove and began to roar, and out of habit, both of them moved to close the damper. Cale got there first. The thump of the damper into place sounded like a thunderclap.

Cale straightened, a frown forming between his eyebrows. "You mean—all this time—" He stopped, as though he were finishing both sentences in his head. "You're in love with Ruby?"

"*Ja*. I don't know what to do. If she goes with your family— if she chooses you—I'll never see her again."

"Does she know?"

"I've been trying to tell her, and I just can't seem to do it right. Tonight is my last chance. All these chores you all are suddenly being asked to do? That's my family, trying to help. Clearing the field, so to speak."

Cale stared, then, shaking his head, he chuckled. "I wondered if all this activity for Old Christmas was normal out here."

"It is earlier in the week. All this extra stuff tonight is for me."

"That's some kind of family you've got."

"I know. But I can't let it go on. It feels dishonest, if your feelings for Ruby are like mine."

After a moment, Cale said, "I don't know if they are." When Zach looked up, he added, "How can they be, after only two weeks? Two weeks, compared with half your life. I mean, I honestly do like her. I was more than willing to give things a chance—to see where they might go. But..." He fell silent.

"Mamm thinks you're on the rebound."

Cale blew out a long breath. "Ouch. Guess my love life isn't as private as I thought."

"I don't know any details. But my mother is pretty experienced when it comes to courtship, what with the last year we've had. She's got a good eye for people."

"Like a hawk. So ... you'll call off the family, and then what?"

Zach pretended to consider. "The two of us march over to the bishop's and ask Ruby to pick one?"

Cale gripped his shoulder in a gesture that was surprisingly brotherly. "She'd probably take a broom to us. No, I think you should go over there alone. I know how I would feel if you came to the Island and started making eyes at Mi—at a girl I liked. It's not a *gut* feeling."

"You're sure?" He could hardly believe it. When had Cale the Competition turned into Cale the Companion, someone who understood?

"Your *mamm* is right, you know. I got dumped pretty hard and I feel like a rubber ball, rebounding off any solid object. Like I can't find my feet." He gazed into the flames through the woodstove's window. "I thought I had my whole life mapped out, and then—"

"Maybe *der Herr* has other ideas," Zach suggested. "You should ask Him."

"You sound like my sister. Both of them."

"*Schweschdere* can be pretty smart. Mine are. We're lucky in our sisters, you and me."

"We're lucky in our families." Cale held out a hand. "I shouldn't say that. Our bishop has probably heard that word on the wind and will call me on the carpet for it when I get home. He doesn't believe in luck."

Zach shook his hand. One firm motion that seemed to cement their relationship on a new and different level. "Luck is just *Gott* working out his will. I guess He got our attention."

"I guess He did. Let us know when the wedding is, okay?"

Zach didn't know whether to grin or blush. Probably he was doing both at this moment. "Come on. I hear chairs scraping upstairs. If we don't hurry, we'll have to sit at the kids' table."

THE NIGHT BEFORE OLD CHRISTMAS WAS A PEACEFUL TIME in the bishop's household. The day had been busy with baking and cooking for tomorrow, but now, after dinner, the family were settled at puzzles or curled up with books, or simply talking quietly and letting their food digest. Ruby was putting the last of the dishes away when a soft knock came at the kitchen door.

Zach. Her heart lifted, and then fell with a thump. No, probably Cale.

And if her heart was behaving like this now, what was it going to do the day after tomorrow, when the time came to leave and she would spend weeks in his company?

She opened the door to find Zach outside in the mud room. At her sharply indrawn breath, he grinned. "*Guder owed*, Ruby."

"I didn't expect to see you." Which was the truth. She hadn't laid eyes on him in over a week—the longest bunch of days that had ever dragged their weary tails across a calendar.

"I know. But I have to talk to you, and tomorrow will be busy, so I thought I would try tonight."

"There's nowhere to talk in here that isn't full of people." Except for her bedroom, but that was completely impossible without walking up the stairs with him in front of the whole family. And she could just imagine what Dat would say.

"It's not too bad outside—it's clouding over. We could go for a walk."

She gazed at him as she leaned on the closed kitchen door, the cool air in the mud room settling on her sleeves and face. Going for walks was what courting couples did. But the two of them had been walking and hiking all over the foothills since they were *Kinner*. There had been no extra significance to it. Maybe there wasn't now, either. Maybe he just wanted to catch up after a busy week.

How depressing. "What do you have to talk about that you can't say right here?"

"Something that doesn't involve you freezing to death. Okay, no walk, then. How about we put some wood in the stove downstairs?"

Mamm had asked one of her grandsons to do it, but he'd been distracted by an animal puzzle and she'd meant to do it herself once the dishes were done. She sighed. "All right."

She lit a lamp, and he followed her downstairs to the basement, where, like most of the Amish homes in the valley, there was a dry woodpile neatly stacked against an outer wall to provide a little extra insulation. While she hung the lamp on its hook, he opened the stove and chose several likely pieces that would provide a good bed of coals for the "keeper," or the big chunk that would last all night.

Once he closed and latched the door, they would need to wait for the wood to catch and get going properly before they shut the damper and went upstairs. He knew as well as she did that they had about ten minutes.

But at least it was toasty warm.

"I had an interesting talk tonight with Cale," he began, closing the stove door and dusting off his hands. "We were putting some wood on, just like this, and he said that he really liked you, but he didn't know how you felt about him."

Good gravy. Ruby squashed the urge to run so she didn't have to hear any more. Was he here to speak on Cale's behalf, the way Emily had asked if her brother could drive her home from singing? Surely not. She didn't think she could stand it.

He glanced at her, as though she ought to respond somehow. But words had deserted her.

"So I told him I didn't know, either. I only knew how I felt. I said I'd been in love with you half my life, and if you went away with them day after tomorrow, I didn't know what I'd do."

The words entered her ears. Her brain. Then her body. Her very being seemed to reverberate the way the air did before you saw a waterfall.

"For the last two days I've been working on this." He pulled a rolled-up piece of paper from his coat pocket. "I know I'm not the greatest talker in the world. And sometimes I'm not even very good at drawing. But Ruby, if you'd look at this, it will tell you everything I want to say."

She took it, but didn't unroll it. Another drawing. Another gift to build her up and then smash her down because she hadn't understood. A rushing river of emotion was building inside her, pushing at the icy control she always had to impose on herself when she was with him—the relentless schooling of her tongue so she wouldn't burst out and tell him how she felt.

She must not speak. If she did—

Her control cracked with an almost audible sound.

"Why are you breaking my heart?" she demanded. "Why, Zach? What did I ever do to make you hurt me like this?"

"Hurt—" He gasped. "The last thing I want to do is hurt you. I love you. I always have."

"But why tell me that when you don't want to marry me?"

"Of course I want to marry you!"

"But you said—the picture of the skaters—you *said*—"

"I was wrong. My tongue got tangled up and everything came out wrong. Please, Ruby. Just look at this."

Her breathing was coming hard. Fast. Her hands quivered, enough to make the paper shake a little as she unrolled it.

She turned so the light from the lamp fell on it.

Her breath caught.

A house so beautiful it could have come out of her own dreams. The aspens, their leaves like a handful of gold coins. She knew exactly where it was situated—they'd all been up there hiking and picnicking. There were the living room windows, which would overlook the river valley so that a person could see the lights of the other homes on the Circle M. But what were these circles? She peered at one. *Ruby's sewing room.* The next—*Zach and Ruby's room. Children's rooms. Kitchen.*

Zach and Ruby's room. Seen from above.

With a bed and a dresser, and built-in bookshelves under the window. The tiny dresser even had a *Kapp* sitting on it, the strings dangling over the edge.

Of all the things that had happened this winter, it was the image of that little *Kapp*—just a few tiny strokes—that did her in.

The shards of her self control went whirling away on the

waterful of emotion overwhelming her, and she burst into tears.

"I've been—so unhappy—" she sobbed. The picture rolled itself up in one hand. "All I want is to be your *wife* and—all I got was Cale and Gideon and they never left me *alone*—and I've been *so miserable!*" She pounded on his chest with one fist, the other careful not to crumple the picture.

His arms came around her and he pulled her against him, her fists still beating weakly over his heart. "*Ach, Liewi*, my sweet Ruby, I'm so sorry. I'm such a dunce. I swear I'll spend the rest of my life learning the right words so that we never misunderstand each other again."

"You're not a dunce," came out of her, crossly, muffled against his coat. "Don't call *mei Mann* names."

His chuckle was a bass note against her cheek. "Forgive me?"

She knew her Zach. He was asking forgiveness for far more than just some name-calling. "In a minute. I'm really upset with you."

"That makes two of us. But did you mean it, Ruby? All you want is what I want? The two of us, in the house we'll build, making a home for ourselves, for our family, and for *Gott?*"

After the hot rush of her feelings, her heart was a gooey blob, especially when he tipped her face up with a fingertip and she met those dear eyes, deep and brown and full of love. For her. Only her. Always her.

"That's all I want," she whispered. "All I've ever wanted. We're going to jump straight from best friends to partners, Zach, just like your little skaters. I've been courting you half my life. And loving you longer."

And then his lips came down on hers, a perfect fit. She had always known they would be. It was like coming home to the one place in all the world where she felt completely safe, completely beloved. It was the past of friendship—the present of newly discovered love—the future that held marriage and family.

It was everything, all in his kiss.

Wrapped in his arms, she still held his drawing in one hand. Carefully, against his back. A picture of their future, and their hearts' home.

EPILOGUE
VENTANA VALLEY, NM

FOUR WINDS RANCH
January 21

DEAR SISTER NAOMI,

We've been home for almost two weeks, so I suppose it's time to find a minute to answer yours. Yes, we had a good trip back, except for a little fuss with the bus going into a snowdrift and the bus company having to send another. But I've learned to expect the unexpected when I travel in the winter.

So your Zach and Ruby have seen the light, have they? Poor Gideon. He'll be disappointed, but he's young enough to get over it pretty quickly. I wouldn't have believed it of quiet Zach, jumping straight from friend to fiancé with no courtship in between! Kids these days, hey?

I'm glad Lorne was able to cancel Ruby's ticket for that trip. My goodness, what a long way to go, on trains and buses and who knows what all. But I'm glad the Kuepfers came to the Circle M. It's good to stay in touch and keep the family lines open. I like Salome, and Lorne has always been one of your favorite cousins, making him one of mine, too. His mother and yours being sisters means you ought to keep them close at heart.

I hope you're sitting down, because I have some news. We weren't home but two days when Tobias and I went to see that young Realtor about putting the ranch up for sale. He hadn't even come out to the 4 Winds to take his photographs and fly his mechanical camera on wings around the property, when he got an offer! The property next to ours has had an absentee owner for as long as I can remember, which is why we leased the grazing rights. Said owner has apparently died, and the property bought by some retired movie person who has lots of money and a conscience about land use. So if I accept, he'll double the size of his spread and pay me a fair bit more than I had thought to ask. How do you like that?

Susanna says that if I needed any more signs that God wanted us in the Siksika, this should convince me. What I see is enough to pay off the mortgage here and buy the Wild Rose Amish Inn. I'll put a little by for my old age, and then renovate the place properly—no cutting corners. I'm thinking you'll see my smiling face on the first of March, if the good Lord wills it. Then we'll hoe right in and get to work. If you'll ask your Noah to write up a list of what he needs to start, maybe Reuben can open accounts for me with the lumberyard and the hardware store.

I can hardly believe so many changes have come in such a short time. I don't know whether to be thankful or not that my boys and Susanna haven't shown an inclination to settle just yet. One part of me wants weddings and grandchildren. Another part is grateful they're happy to come with me and make a new life in the Siksika.

I'll let this do for now.
Ever your loving
Rachel

. . .

PS: THERE WAS A POSTCARD WAITING AT THE POST OFFICE WHEN we got home, from Luke Hertzler. Remember him? He was one of Marlon's side-sitters at our wedding. A bit of a flirt then. Sounds like he's had his share of trials and is down on his luck now, poor man. I haven't seen him since Tobias was born. I did hear something tragic happened, just no details. Well, if he plans to drop in, I hope he does it before the end of February.

See you soon—RM

THE END

AFTERWORD
NOTE FROM ADINA

I hope you've enjoyed the sixth book about the Miller family on the Circle M Ranch. If you subscribe to my newsletter, you'll hear about new releases in the series, my research in Montana, and snippets about quilting and writing and chickens—my favorite subjects! You'll find the subscription page on my website, adinasenft.com

Turn the page for a glossary of the Pennsylvania Dutch words used in this book. But first, here's a sneak peek at *The Amish Cowboy's Refuge*, the first book in a new miniseries featuring Rachel Miller and her family, now part of The Amish Cowboys of Montana series!

THE AMISH COWBOY'S REFUGE © ADINA SENFT

Second chances are God's way of telling us to try again. —Mountain Home Amish proverb

Rachel Miller has sold her ranch in New Mexico and returned to the Montana valley where she grew up. Where she fell in love. Where she married the man she wanted to grow old with. But life brings changes, and she's returning a widow. She buys a dilapidated inn in Mountain Home, which she plans to renovate and restore with the help of her four grown children and her extended family on the Circle M Ranch.

Long ago, Luke Hertzler was the best friend of Rachel's late husband. But his life hasn't been an easy one, and now he's just a cowhand for hire, with a past that dogs every wandering step. When he learns Rachel needs help if the Wild Rose Amish Inn is to open on time, all he can offer her are two hands, a hammer, and hard work. Then he'll move on like he always does.

Can a broken wanderer find redemption in the home of a woman who needs to sink her roots deep into the land? And can a widow learn that even later in life, her heart is big enough to love again?

The Montana Millers. They believe in faith, family, and the land. They'll need all three when love comes to Mountain Home!

Find your copy of The Amish Cowboy's Refuge at your favorite online retailer!

GLOSSARY

Spelling and definitions from Eugene S. Stine, *Pennsylvania German Dictionary* (Birdboro, PA: Pennsylvania German Society, 1996).

Words used:
   Aendi: auntie
   Bischt du okay? Are you okay?
   Boppli(n): baby, babies
   Bruder: brother
   Daadi: grandfather
   Daadi Haus: grandfather house
   Dat: Dad
   deemiedich: humble
   Demut: humility
   denki: thanks
   Docher: daughter
   Dochdere: daughters
   Eck: corner, esp wedding table
   Englisch: not-Amish people, English language

der Herr: the Lord

Frehlicher Grischdaag: Merry Christmas

Gmee: congregation, community

Gott: God

Grossdaadi: great-grandfather

Grossmammi: great-grandmother

Guder abend: Good afternoon/evening

Guder mariye: Good morning

Guder nacht: Good night

gut: good

hoch Deitsch: high German

Ischt okay? Is it okay?

ja: yes

Kaffee: coffee

Kapp: women's prayer covering

Kind, Kinner: child, children

kumm mit: come along

Liewi: dear

Maedsche(r): girl, girls

Mamm: Mom

Mammi: Grandma

Mann: man

mei: my

mei Fraa: my wife

Mei Vater, hilfe mich. My Father, help me.

Narre: idiots

narrisch: crazy

neh: no

Neuwesitzer(n): side-sitter(s), the bridal couple's supporter

Nix? Is it not?

Onkel: uncle

Ordnung: discipline, or standard of behavior and dress unique to each community

Schweschder(e): sister(s)

Sohn: son

Uffrohr: uproar

Wie geht's? How's it going?

wunderbaar: wonderful

Youngie: young people

Balm of Gilead

The Longest Road

The Highest Mountain

The Sweetest Song

The Heart's Return (novella)

Smoke River

Grounds to Believe

Pocketful of Pearls

The Sound of Your Voice

Over Her Head

Glory Prep (faith-based young adult)

Glory Prep

The Fruit of My Lipstick

Be Strong and Curvaceous

Who Made You a Princess?

Tidings of Great Boys

The Chic Shall Inherit the Earth

facebook.com/adinasenft

x.com/shelleyadina

pinterest.com/shelleyadina

bookbub.com/authors/adina-senft

instagram.com/shelleyadinasenft

ABOUT THE AUTHOR

USA Today bestselling author Adina Senft grew up in a plain house church, where she was often asked by outsiders if she was Amish (the answer was no). She holds a PhD in Creative Writing from Lancaster University in the UK. Adina was the winner of RWA's RITA Award for Best Inspirational Novel in 2005, a finalist for that award in 2006, and was a Christy Award finalist in 2009. She appeared in the 2016 documentary film *Love Between the Covers*, is a popular speaker and convention panelist, and has been a guest on many podcasts, including Worldshapers and Realm of Books.

She writes steampunk adventure and mystery as Shelley Adina; and as Charlotte Henry, writes classic Regency romance. When she's not writing, Adina is usually quilting, sewing historical costumes, or enjoying the garden with her flock of rescued chickens.

Adina loves to talk with readers about books, quilting, and chickens!
www.adinasenft.com
adinasenft@comcast.net